A River Called Heaven

by

Scotland Payne

A River Called Heaven

ISBN — 0-9792847-0-8
ISBN — 978-0-9792847-0-0

Typeset by GW Associates in Times New Roman 12/16

Printed in the United States of America

Acknowledgments

This book would not have been possible without the help and support of my many friends in the La Mesa writing class. Thanks to: Joe Toricelli for introducing me to the class; Book Coach Judy Collins who took me under her wing; Linda Smith for putting up with my bad spelling; Graham Warden for his patient advice; Sharon, always there to help and encourage me; The African American Writers and Artists, Inc. for their input; and my partner, Woo, who over coffee kept me on track.

The Author

Scotland Payne has retired from his government job and lives in San Diego, California. He lived through the tough and time-changing world he writes about, and often visits his beloved Tryon and Blue Ridge Mountain region where he has kin and many friends.

He is now working on his second novel about War and Fox as secret agents.

Email the author at: vettee@aol.com
Or call 619-200-2595

1
A River Called Heaven

The year is 1964, and African-Americans are still called 'Colored' and Negro men, regardless of their age, are called 'boys'. Negroes can't eat at the lunch counters, drink out of the same fountains or even use the same restrooms as White folks. It's called segregation, and that damn old Jim Crow law in the South is real.

That's the way it is in this small western North Carolina town called Tryon, in the foothills of the Blue Ridge Mountains, whose most famous person is Nina Simone, the singer.

On this special Easter Sunday morning the fresh mountain air is perfumed by the spring blossoms. Tryon is truly a Garden of Eden. As I sit in the Colored Baptist Church looking at a stained glass window showing Jesus holding his staff, a beam of sunlight shines from the tip of the staff, filtering through the stained glass like a spotlight gleaming from Heaven. The minister is preaching about all the saints going there.

But my mind is on our Heaven here, a river deep in the woods, where my uncle and the big boys are supposed to take us after church. We can't swim in the public swimming pool across town with the White people, so we swim in the river. We don't really care because it's more fun and natural than some man-made swimming pool.

The old folks tell us the River Heaven got its name because it felt like heaven to the slaves, who used to slip away out of the hot fields to wade, swim, and even bathe in its cool waters. The river has kept its name to this day.

Daniel Boone's brother, a distant great-grandfather on my mother's side was White. He married a house slave, half-Black and half-Cherokee; their daughter married a man half-White and half-Black. On my father's side, my grandmother is Cherokee and grandpa is Black. I'm lucky—I got the best traits from each race: tall and strong from my Blackness, a light skin color from the Whites, a reddish skin tone and long black hair from the Indians.

No one is sure how it started, but all of us in this rural town of Tryon have nicknames. As the story goes, this tradition may have begun with the slaves, who hated the White man's names so much they gave each other nicknames.

My nickname is War, short for Warrior; I wear my black hair long like a Cherokee brave. Being light-complexioned, I'm a good-looking young boy. I don't look Black, but that doesn't matter in the South. If you have one drop of Black blood in you, you're Black. I also have White and Indian blood in me; I often wonder why I'm not one of them?

Going to an all Black segregated school I used to get in fights with the real dark skinned kids. I later learned they are jealous of me because of my light skin. This is stupid, but there's prejudice between light and dark skinned folks even within the Negro race.

But now I'm almost fourteen. There's something nice about having "teen" in your age. I am a true warrior. After hours of throwing my dagger into the red mud of the Carolina hillsides I have become an expert, and almost always have my dagger with me. I also take martial arts lessons so no one messes with me anymore.

Church service is almost finished now. We're sitting beside this three hundred pound plus lady, the one we helped hide Easter eggs for the little kids. I'm with my best friend, whose nickname is Fox. He's Asian. He came to Tryon in the early fifties, and with his color and dark eyes, people said he was fast and sly like a fox. The name stuck.

2
Pops

His grandfather came here during World War II. Asians caught hell during the war because of the Japanese bombing Pearl Harbor. Since it's so rural here, he figured living on the Negro side of town would cause him fewer problems. It worked; everybody here in Tryon knows his family as just some different looking Negroes.

He made us call him Pops, the nickname of Louis Armstrong, the legendary trumpet player. He loves Louis and often plays his music as he teaches us martial arts. He says the name makes him sound cool and besides he doesn't like to be called Grandpa. He likes to tell the story how Louis and the great jazzman Lionel Hampton went to play for the Pope. "Hamp was jamming, and Louis was scatting. The Pope was bobbing his head and patting his foot. When Louis said to the Pope, 'I see you dig our Jazz, Pops.'"

"Louis," says Lionel, "You can't call the holy Father 'Pops'. He's the head of the Catholic Church." But old Louis did anyway, and the Pope loved it. So if the name is good enough for Louis Armstrong and the Pope, it's good enough for me. Pops has looked on me as a grandson ever since I proved myself, which was not easy.

The first day I went to training, Fox and I run. The first half-mile was easy, a nice jog along a country road. Then we hit the half mile hill, a very steep winding road. We made it to the top, but then headed back on the Olympic Equestrian Trail. In 1960 the Olympic equestrian team came to Tryon to train their jumping horses. Though somewhat raggedy, the Equestrian trail is still here. It took me days before I could finish the run, and couldn't start training until I finished it.

3
Fox

Pops seemed glad when I finally did, because now Fox has a training partner, who just happens to be his best friend.

Fox is two years older than I am, and a martial arts expert. He has a sister my age, named Jade; she is the finest sister in the world. I started training with him hoping to score with her, but instead we became best buddies.

The preacher hits an octave higher now and, all of a sudden, the big lady sitting beside us jumps up and starts to shout. But she's eaten too many Easter eggs and lets out a big fart. We laugh so hard we almost cry and bow down like we're praying to hide our faces.

Church is finally out; so we run to my house to change our Sunday clothes. My house is the closest to the edge of the woods. As we arrive, we see Uncle and the big boys taking off for Heaven. We change quickly and in a short time catch up with them. We've been in the woods many times, even have our own swimming hole in one of the small creeks that run into Heaven. We never go too far because we are afraid there might be bears, or some other animals that might get us.

Walking into the woods we enter a world where only God's creature's voices can be heard, like the sound of a woodpecker beating out a tune on a tree off in the distance. Squirrels make a noise as they leap through the trees, while the wind blows a soft melody through them.

My Cherokee ancestors traveled these woods for thousands of years, leaving only a faint trail. We're walking in their footsteps on the same paths they used not so long ago, hunting and traveling from village to village. I can still feel their presence lingering as we walk along in the same pathways.

My White ancestors with their coonskin caps make another story. I look off to the left, way up on the mountain where they cut down a big part of the forest for lumber. It doesn't seem to matter, though. The forest is so big; what could the cutting hurt?

In a little while we come to the edge of the woods, where it opens up into a big field, the same one my slave ancestors farmed just one hundred years ago. I picture them wearing old clothes and hats as they hoe, sweating as they toil in the fields, while my White ancestor sits on his horse, with his gun in his hand, making sure they don't run away. Off in the distance I can hear Heaven, and my heart beats like a Cherokee drum from excitement.

I look around at the flowering dogwood trees with their pure white blossoms, the mountain laurel, and smell the honeysuckle. Red birds and blue jays sing a joyful tune in the trees. The sky is crystal-clear blue, the spring air perfumed by a soft southern breeze. I wonder if God's heaven with its streets paved with gold and silver can compare with this part of western Carolina in the springtime.

We cross a large field and we come to the river; there are trees all along its bank. Just upstream we hear a waterfall, and around the bend, the big boys know a place where the high water from heavy rains have cut a big horseshoe curve to make a small sandy beach completely hidden from view. This is where we'll swim.

7

The big boys start taking off their clothes. Fox and I undress real fast. We're in great shape from the martial arts workouts, and proud of our bodies. But watching the big boys undress, I'm shocked. I've never seen grown men completely naked. Their things are really big, and now I know why the White man don't want Negroes messing with their women. The one they nicknamed Candy is so big I wonder how he ever gets any. He got his nickname from an old blues song called "Candy Man," about a well-endowed blues singer. I'm looking at their things. To my surprise, they're all different sizes and shapes, just like people—one slightly curved, another short and fat, one skinny and one very small.

Smiling, Fox whispers in my ear, "At least all you Negroes ain't blessed down there."

I see Fox fly into the river, then I feel a jab under my arms, and into the river I go. The water's ice-cold, but that's the least of my problems. I can't swim! I hit bottom. Remembering Tarzan in the movies, I push off from the sandy bottom. As I reach the top, kicking and stroking, I hear the big boys laughing.

Fox can swim and seems to be enjoying himself, as I struggle to make it to the bank. In my mind, soon as I get to my dagger, some big boy's gonna die for throwing me in the water. Splashing and kicking, I pull up on the bank. I'm laughing now, happy because I swam and forget I'm mad at the big boys.

The big boys swim while Fox and I sit on the sand and make fun of their private parts as they come out of the cold water. They're all shriveled up like old prunes. Even Candy's is only about an inch long.

4
Sun

On May first, the whole school turns out to march around the May Day flagpole. I watch the young girls weave the red, white, and blue streamers over and under, turning the pole into a colorful work of art. School will be out soon, and we'll be free for what I hope will be a great summer. Next fall I leave Tryon to go up north to high school in the big city. But this summer I plan to have lots of fun.

School lets out early so Fox and I meet up with another buddy we call Sun. Sun's Uncle Ben was a World War II hero. He lost his arm in the war, and always wore his Purple Heart, Silver Star, and his others medals.

Ben, a true militant and a pain in the White people's behind, is always telling them how he froze his butt off in the bitter cold and killed plenty of Germans in the big war. Now he has to watch Germans eat lunch in a restaurant he can't even go into. He lost his arm fighting for his country, but still can't use the same restroom as White folks. The White folks feel mighty uneasy around him, until their Ku Klux Klan get him one night. Ben earned the dubious distinction of being the last known Negro lynched in the area.

Sun really hates White people and says he's taking over where his Uncle Ben left off. To make matters worse, some old White man's doing it to his mother. Sun's always talking about how he's gonna show the Negro the light when he grows up and take them out of the darkness of ignorance into the bright light, like the sun. That's why we gave him the nickname Sun. We call ourselves "The Three Musketeers," whenever he catches up with Fox and me.

We tell him about Heaven and how nice it is to swim there.

Sun says the water should be warm now, and the fish are biting, so off to Heaven we head. On our way we meet another of our friends. He has a long head like a football, with nappy hair that rolls up like little BBs, so we call him Head. When we get to Heaven, we put our clothes on the bank and wade a little ways downstream. The water now is bathtub warm from the May sun.

Sun has a big burlap sack in his hand, but we have no idea what he's going to do with it. Shortly after, we come to a shallow part of the river. Sun puts the sack on one side of a big rock and tells us to jab the other side with a stick. We jab, and all the fish run into the burlap sack. We keep the nice sized ones and put the rest back in the water. After doing this for twenty minutes we have a whole string of fish.

5
Birthday Suits

We're laughing and singing and cutting up when we get back to where we left our clothes. All of that stops, when we look around for our clothes. They're gone. At first we think we're in the wrong place. Then reality sets in—no clothes in the middle of the day. We scamper up the bank to the edge of the road, just in time to see a man in the distance pulling away in his tractor. He has on bib overalls and a long-sleeved shirt. The only thing we can see is the back of his neck, turned red from the sun.

"That damn redneck checker done took our clothes!" Sun hollers. At least he left us all the stuff from our pockets, our keys, my dagger, and our little bit of money. We see Redneck pull into a barn about a half-mile away. We wait, hoping he'll bring our clothes back. But after a while we know there's no hope, so we gather our few things. Sun puts the fish back in the water, and we run as fast as we can across the field into the woods.

It doesn't take us long to learn that the woods without clothes and shoes is a hard place. Our feet are cut and hurting from running over sticks and rocks, and the bugs are biting in strange places.

When we settle down, Head starts crying. "My mama gonna kill me if I come home with no clothes." He's kind of everybody's whipping boy, with his long head and small body. We just let him hang out with us to make him feel good.

"We're just like slaves running from the White boss man. Nothing has changed. He still got his foot up our behind, but he ain't gonna get away with this. Head, you stop whining like a little White boy." He calms down.

"Sun, how you know what a little White boy does?" Fox taunts. "Bet one could whip your behind! Anyway, why you always downing White people? Some of them are good, like, you know…right now I can't think of any. Oh yea! I know one—our Carolina brother, Billy Graham."

Sun kind of laughs and says, "You just like us, just a different-looking Negro. You might not have any Colored blood in you, but you can't go to his school, eat in his res'rant, or mess with his women, and yo' ass is runnin' round out here in the woods in your birthday suit just like us! And who did it to us, in case you forgot? The redneck-ass White man!"

I tell them to stop bickering so we can figure out what we're going to do. Not far from where we are, there's a small stone house the Cherokee Indians built many years ago. It sits right on a stream, so we head for it. The naked butt looks real funny at first as I walk behind Sun and Head looking at their backsides, but after a while their butts just look natural, like any other part of the body. The thought runs through my head that if everyone was naked, man wouldn't think so high of himself.

We get to the stone house and look inside.

Fox says, "Look at the water. It's running from a spring into two small channels along each side of the wall."

The Indians used to put their meat and anything they wanted to keep it cool and safe from coons, opossums, and even black bears. It's unbelievable, but after all these years, the spring water still runs at the same speed. The top of the house and the front door are long gone, but it's still cool inside. The Cherokee Indians had made a natural icebox. The hardest thing is finding a place to sit. The leaves stick to your behind, or it feels like bugs crawling up your butt, even when there are none. We rest our feet in the little creek that runs along the side of the stone springhouse.

"This cool water sure is soothing my tired and hurting feet from all the sticks and stones I stepped on. I understand now why the slaves named the river Heaven, 'cause this water sho' feels like heaven to my sore feet," Head says. He bobs his feet up and down, making a splashing sound.

Although none of us is getting any, we start telling lies about who said they were gonna give us some.

"Y'all need to stop lying. Ain't nobody gonna give y'all nothing," Head says. "Let me tell you about Cassius Clay whipping Sonny Liston's ass last February in Charlotte. I saw it on TV. He TKO'd Liston in the eighth round, then talked bad about the man calling him a big ugly bear, and too ugly to whip him. Clay is one bad mother. I bet he could even whip Joe Louis' ass."

Head shadow-boxes around with his little thing bouncing up and down imitating Cassius, flowing like a butterfly and stinging like a bee.

Sun gets up, wades out in the stream and starts peeing in the water when this big horsefly buzzes around his head. He looks so funny swinging at that horsefly and peeing in the stream at the same time, we fall out laughing.

We decide to wait till dark to slip up to my house so I can get some clothes for them to wear home. Getting used to being naked and telling lies, other than being a little hungry, we feel kind of happy.

Sun cocks his head and listens, "Y'all hear that?" he says. A kind of cracking sound rumbles away off in the distance. The sky gets dark, and the wind picks up. We hear it coming, far off in the trees. Just what we don't need—rain.

We run for a cut in the bank, a small cave some animal must have dug. We get under it just as the rain arrives, and the drops echo through the trees like small drums. We sit there as the rain takes center stage. No more animal sounds, no birds singing. The rain plays a symphony, a kind of music you can only hear when it's absolutely quiet. The drops are falling from the trees, "pitter-patter," upon the leaves on the ground. The water rushes by like a small stream and the smell of rain in the woods gives us an invigorating, uplifting clean feeling.

But shortly Sun has us all laughing as he hollers out, "We all Neanderthal Niggers! That's all we are! Neanderthal Niggers, with no clothes, no women, no food, just sitting in this hole like Black cave men. This Oriental Nigger! This half-breed Nigger and this Nigger with a long head. We still all Neanderthal Niggers!"

A little while later, it's so peaceful and quiet we fall asleep. When we wake up it is almost dark, and still raining, so we brave the rain and make it to the edge of the woods. There's no moon, and it's pitch black. Under the cover of darkness we slip to my house. We're lucky it's raining, and not many people are out. We never lock our doors, so I easily go into the house, give my friends enough clothes and coats to get home, and off they go. All things considered, it's been a good day.

6
Movies

Saturday matinee at the movies is double-feature day. A great western is playing—*Broken Arrow*—with Jeff Chandler as the great Apache Indian chief "Cochise" and Jimmy Stewart, as "Tom Jeffords" the great White friend of the Apache nation.

Popcorn is a quarter, and it's thirty-five cents for a ticket if you are twelve or under. The man won't let me get by as under twelve any more, so I pay the adult fare of fifty-five cents and head upstairs to the balcony, where the Colored folks sit. It's "Whites Only" down below. There's a rumor going around that the Civil Rights law is going to pass this year, and we'll be able to sit anywhere. If it does, knowing us, we'll still stay up here.

Broken Arrow is a great movie. Everybody's still. Even the men are about to cry when the White man shoots and kills Jimmy Stewart's Apache Indian wife.

Sun breaks the silence. "See? The White man not only fucks up the Negroes, he fucks up the Indian, too. Men, women, children, dogs, he don't give a good fuck. He'll kill a rock if it's red or black!" But no one laughs, for the movie has made us sad, and besides, we all know Sun is a little bit off and how much he hates White folks.

The second movie is the one that causes all the trouble. It's a comedy about a haunted house. An old White man and his wife see this ghost, and take off real fast in their car. The speedometer shows sixty-five miles an hour when the butler,

15

a real big-eyed Black man named Stepin Fetchit, sees the ghost and takes off running. With his arms pumping and head back, he passes the White couple in their car. Some White person from below hollers, "Look at that Nigger run!" Another one says, "Run, you pop-eyed Nigger! Run!"

Sun can't stand it any longer. He gets up and leans over the balcony with a big cup of ice from his drink. "Run wit' this, Cracker!" he yells, throwing it over the balcony. Now other people start throwing popcorn boxes and cups over the balcony.

The White boys down below gather together, hollering "We're coming up there and kick some Black ass!" They start out the door. The balcony is so silent you could hear a rat pee on cotton.

My favorite big boy, Candy, says, "The White boys are mad, not so much because of the trash we threw over, but because next year Negroes will be attending their school. They're losing their way of life. Once we were their slaves, just pieces of property, then we moved up to second-class citizens, but soon we'll be first class citizens. We can sit by the White girls, and look at their butts, and 'accidentally on purpose' bump into them in the hallway without getting hung. Those White boys are mad as hornets, just looking for an excuse to fight. When they come up here I am gonna break my finger off pointing at you. Sun, you gonna get your ass kicked!"

We hear the door open and the White boys running up the steps. When they get to the top, it is graveyard quiet. A big two-hundred-pound-plus White boy hollers, "Which one of you Black-ass Niggers threw popcorn on me?" No one speaks at first.

"We did, if you don't like it come on over here and take this ass-whipping I'm gonna put on your Cracker ass," Sun says. Slowly Sun slides behind Fox and me. The big White boy doesn't waste any time in his rush to punch Fox. That's his big mistake. Fox has been into martial arts since he was two. His grandfather was the champion of Asia, and at sixteen he says Fox is even better than he was. I've gotten almost as good, training over a year every day except Sunday and holidays or bad weather.

Fox blocks the punch and hits the boy with several quick punches. The big White boy gets a strange look on his face, and falls like a giant oak tree. But there are several more White boys, and I jump into the pile punching and kicking. I remember Pops teaching us how not to panic and how not to throw any deadly punches. Fox and I both could seriously hurt someone with one punch, if we choose. We knew the right pressure points to hit to take someone out. I hit one boy with a strike on his shoulder and his whole side went numb. This is not the time for serious strikes. We're both mowing guys down without hitting any vital spots.

Now I understand why after every workout, Pops has us spend five minutes dodging the tall cane he always carries in the dojo—a karate training place. He swings it at our feet and we have to jump over it, or he jabs it at us, and we have to parry or duck it. I see a fist coming toward my face and I duck, and then punch where it comes from. After dodging Pop's cane in the dojo, this is easy.

Someone yells, "Police!" and, just like someone had pushed a button, everybody streams to their seats. The movie stops.

The lights are already on as the Sheriff comes down the

aisle with his gun drawn, "Somebody's going to jail! Which one of you Niggers started this?"

White boys are moaning in the aisles. The Sheriff asks again, "Where are all the people that beat up these boys?" One of the White boys lying on the floor points at Fox and me. The Sheriff says, "Stan' up, you two, and all the rest that helped." But no one moves. The Sheriff looks around. "Someone better speak up," he roars.

"Sheriff, we just trying to watch the movie, when those bullies come up here and jump on those two young boys for no reason. You should get those bullies off the floor, Sheriff, and take them to jail," Candy says.

"Let me get this straight. You mean to tell me those two boys beat up all these people? Y'all must think I'm a damn fool, or crazy or something."

"No, Sheriff. Them two boys, they sho' can fight."

The Sheriff looks at us.

"What kinda Colored are you all, anyway? One looks like a Jap or Chinaman, and the other is yellow with long black hair. By God, you all half-breeds or something?" He tilts his head over at Candy. "You mean they really beat up all these boys?" He looks back at us. "Everybody get out. The movie is closed down." Everyone leaves in a hurry, except the White boys. Some still lie in the aisles, moaning.

We head to the storefront where all the fellows hang out—old, young and in-between. In this small town, it's the gathering place. Some of the big boys work as porters on the trains, and some work for rich White people, but most of them work in the hotel as cooks or waiters, and they all end up at the storefront after work.

The fellows sit on the long rows of concrete steps and

drink beer. Some of the old men drink their white lightning out of Mason jars wrapped in brown paper bags, in case the police happen to ride by, while others shoot penny dice in the corner. "Baby needs a new pair of shoes, fever in the funk house, eight shake and donate," they holler while rolling the dice. As if losing a few pennies would kill them.

But now we are the heroes. All the talk is about us, about how Fox and I beat not six or eight, but thirty or forty men and turned out the movie. The big boys are offering to buy us anything we want, RC Cola, Nehi Grape, moon pies, even my favorite soda, Nehi Strawberry. The young girls are smiling like they want to give us some. Life is good.

7
Trying to Get Some

All night long it rained "cats and dogs", as the old folks used to say. When it's time for our run, the rain that held us up all morning stops. The air is sweet, cool and clean. As I arrive at Fox's house he is waiting, ready to go. In the early part of our run we come to Jolene's house. She is pretty with her light-brown skin, tall, and she has a well-put-together body. Fox is in love with her and so are half of Tryon. She's a straight-A student, studies music and teaches Sunday school. She and Fox's sister, Jade, are kind of the untouchable girls in Tryon.

As we run past, Jolene and her girlfriend stand outside on the porch in shorts. Fox looks at them and gets his foot all tangled up with mine. He trips and falls to the ground. Jolene comes down and asks if he's hurt.

He gets up slowly. "My arm feels like it's broken," he moans while trying to keep a straight face.

"Po' baby," she coos. "Please come up on the porch and let me put some ice on it, and rub it for you." As we walk up onto the porch she tells her girlfriend to go make some lemonade, and Jolene sits Fox down in the swing.

I'm looking at her friend's behind as she walks into the house to make the lemonade. She's older, about seventeen, and her name is Rebecca. She is shoe-polish black, short with a big butt and shapely legs, real earthy, just the opposite of Jolene, who is refined and sophisticated, at least for Tryon.

Jolene's father works for the Vanderbilt's, one of the richest families in the world. It's said they looked all over the States and found this to be the most beautiful part of the country. Then they built the Biltmore House in Asheville, with over two-hundred rooms. They take good care of Jolene's father financially.

I sit down on the porch and watch as Jolene rubs Fox's arm and talks about how hard his muscles are.

Rebecca comes out with the lemonade. "Come and get it," she says, setting it on a small table.

When we go to get our drinks, Fox doesn't get up. He has this big hard-on, which he's trying to hide by covering the front of his pants with his hand. Both girls look at him and laugh. Jolene says, "It looks like more than your arm muscle is hard." Laughing, she gets up and gets a glass for him, then sits back down in the swing. After a while they go into the house.

Rebecca is leaning back, her breasts sticking out like six-shooters and her legs opening and closing like she's fanning her stuff. It dawns on me there are no grown-ups around. Maybe this could be the first time I get some.

"You wanna go and lay down?" I ask in a shaky voice.

"I don't care," she says.

We get up and go in and sit on the bed. She leans over and kisses me. Now I have a big hard-on. I start playing with her titties and put my hand in her panties to play with her stuff, like I've heard the big boys talk about. She is breathing hard and pulls her shorts and panties down and stretches out on the bed. As I go to put it in, I remember my grandmother, who is fair-skinned, "light-bright and almost white," as the saying goes. She told me," Stay away from

Black girls because they'll put a spell on you. Never go with anyone darker than a brown paper bag." I remember her telling me one time that a Black girl down in South Carolina put a hex on our light skinned cousin, James, and every full moon he goes up on a hill, barks and howls at the moon like a coyote all night long. "So, you had better leave the Black girls alone."

But the big boys always say, "The blacker the berry, the sweeter the juice," and I'm about to find out who is right. I try to put it in. I push hard, because the talk is she's screwing one of the big boys and I figure it will go in easy but it doesn't. The hair around her stuff is coarse and hurts my thing. I am about to give up on Black girls when she guides me into her and I feel her opening up. She's hot, wet and tight. She's moaning, and breathing hard.

"Easy, easy. You're hurting me," she says.

Nothing in my life has ever come close to feeling this good.

Just then a car pulls into the driveway. Fox comes running in.

"Let's go! Let's go!" He hollers. But this stuff is feeling just too good and I can't make myself get up. He has to pull me off the girl. I look down and see blood. She was a virgin, and so was I. As we run out the back door and up the hill I know the big boys are right. "The blacker the berry, the sweeter the juice."

On our way home, Fox says how fine Jolene is, with her long legs and tall shapely body. "She told me she's been looking at me and wanted to talk to me for a long time, but I was too shy to say anything to her.

"I am so much in love with her, but mad as hell because

she won't give me any. She just keeps saying she's a lover of the Lord and wants more than sex in her life. She says we can be girlfriend and boyfriend if I want. And believe me I want to, even if she ain't givin' it up yet."

Fox and I part, and when I get home I am so happy. I got to put my thing in some and it sure felt good even if I didn't finish. I am growing up.

Late June, the Southern days are hot, with the temperature in the nineties, and the humidity even higher. We move our workouts to seven in the morning. The next morning, bright and early, I open Pops' gate and wait in the front yard for Fox and Pops to come out so we can begin our workouts like I always do.

8
Asian Life-Style

F ox comes to the door and motions for me to come in.
This is a total surprise. I have never been in their
house, mostly because they make Jade stay in the house
while we workout. Their house is the only one in the
Colored section that is completely fenced in so no one can
see into the back yard. Shortly I will know why.

As I enter, Fox asks me to remove my shoes. Without
thinking I do, and step on a work of art, a warm colorful
Oriental rug. Brightly colored paintings of Asian art hang on
the walls. My jaw drops, for I only know white and black
and north and south. I find myself in a completely different
culture, a room straight out of Asia, right in the heart of this
small Southern town.

Fox shows me how they have chambers running from the
stove under the floor to keep it warm in the winter, because
no one wears shoes in the house. I ask why, and Fox says,
"It's traditional. And besides, you step in chicken or dog
mess, or worse, and bring it right into your house if you keep
your shoes on."

Walking out the back door, I find some sandals to slip on.
I walk into the most captivating park-like setting I have ever
seen. It looks like a replica of the Garden of Eden with a
small waterfall, and pond full of exotic colorful fish in an
array of colors. White, gold, gray, orange, white flecked
with orange and black, they look like swimming art.

"The fish are carp called Koi," Fox says.

My knees get weak as I look over and see Jade kneeling in front of a statue of Buddha, praying. She has her native dress on, purple with a yellow design of a dragon running through it. Her hair is long and full, not tied back in the two ponytails like she wears to school. She's turning from a little girl into a beautiful young lady.

Pops is over in the corner doing karate in slow motion.

"What's he doing?" I ask Fox.

"Pops is doing tai chi, and Jade is chanting to Buddha, her God."

Those two things I knew nothing about. This Asian lifestyle is full of pleasant surprises.

Fox explains and points out things in the garden, like Pops' bonsai display of miniaturized plants. I hardly hear him. I watch as Jade gets up and comes toward us. We're standing by the pond, and as she walks by, she pushes me right into it. This water is not like Heaven. It has a funky fishy smell from the Koi. As I hurry to get out, Pops laughs out of control. So does Fox.

Jade disappears into the house, and Pops comes over, still laughing. He tells us to go get in the dojo for a light workout. I ask Fox why Jade pushed me in the water.

"Jolene told her about Rebecca," he is laughing. "She's mad as hell at you."

"Why do you let Jolene do that? You're supposed to be my boy. Can't you handle your women and make her keep her trap shut?" I ask.

"You know they are friends. Don't be hollering at me 'cause you got busted. Come on! We'd better get around to the dojo, before Pops gets mad. Then he'll work our butts off."

9
The Damn Adam Test

We get in the dojo, but this time Pops comes out and lays his cane on the grass.

"Before your workout, I want to talk to you," he says. "This is a one-time talk, so I want your full attention. I want every answer to be well thought out before you give it. Understand?"

We both bow our heads and say we understand.

"There are very few men in the world today," Pops says, "who can beat either one of you in a fight, and soon there may be none. I studied under some of Asia's greatest Grand Masters and became one of its greatest fighters. I see things in you two that are better than anything in me. I have taught you martial arts secrets only a few Masters know. These are secret techniques, many that never will leave Asia. Grandsons, you know things about the martial arts you don't even realize you know. I have gladly taught you and never asked anything in return. But now I am asking two things. Do you agree to them?"

We look at each other, but don't answer.

"I see you are smart enough," Pops grins, "to get the question before you give the answer. I have been watching your sparring sessions lately, and they are getting more combative, almost like you want to fight each other, which is good. So here is my first request: I want you to promise me, on your word of honor, that never under any circumstances will you ever fight each other. Some day soon you might wonder which of you is best. Right now we know Fox is, but as War grows bigger and stronger, that can change and it will be hard on you not to put it to the test."

"We would never fight each other anyway. We are like brothers, but I promise," Fox says.

"I promise too, but I could never fight my best buddy," I say.

"Now that is a law in your life. The next thing is that you will have no sex until you are eighteen," Pops says.

We look at each other. All of a sudden this is not funny. I can't wait to finish what I've started with the Black girl, and I could swear I see a tear in Fox's eye. He wants that tall long-legged brown-skinned beauty, as he calls her, and to think he can't get any for almost two more years is like torture, I know.

Pops waits, but there is no answer.

"War, you are so young. Let your body grow and mature. You have a whole lifetime for that." He turns to look at Fox.

"This should be easy for you, Grandson. You'll be eighteen in less than two years."

"Why can't you at least give us some kind of hope? Like maybe only with one girl, or if I break the board?" Fox begs.

"Okay," Pops says. "I'll make it a little easier. War, you can have sex at seventeen with one girl, but not in North or South Carolina. And you, Fox, if you break the board next year at seventeen, you can have sex with one girl too, but not in North or South Carolina. You both go along with that?"

I'm mystified. "What's this…board you talkin' about? We've broken a lot of boards in our training."

Pops goes over and picks one up. He walks back to me and holds it up over his head.

"Now break it," he says. This is a piece of cake as I start to punch it.

"No! With your feet," Pops says, "from a standstill."

I think he's kidding, but he's for real.

"Get out of my way. Let me try," Fox says, as he swings his body back and forth and leaps up, kicking the board, but not breaking it. Then I try, and fall dead on my behind.

"Okay," Pops says. "Get back in the dojo. And do I have your word?"

We look at each other, but neither one of us can say yes.

"I raised Fox and Jade to make up their own minds," Pops goes on talking. "I read to them from all the great religion books, and then Jade converted to Buddhism. That is her course. Fox became a Baptist, I think, mostly because he wants to be with you, War. That is his course. Maybe as they get wiser they will change, or maybe they won't. I am old, and I will die soon." He's looking straight at me now. "But just as I told them, War, I am telling you. You are like my other grandson, a part of this family. If someone harms you they have to harm me also.

"I call my religion the universal truth, because man makes religion, but God's truth is universal. War, in your great book, the Bible, it tells the story of Adam, the perfect man, and how he had the whole world, dominion over everything but this one piece of fruit. God told him not to touch it, but he had to do it anyway."

He shifts his gaze to Fox, then back to me.

"You two are like Adam. You have great bodies from all your training, and very good looks, and I am sure you could get almost any woman you want, because they will be after you. I was young once, and I know how you feel. But there

28

is another part to life, more than just getting some. This is the part you must overcome. The inner man or spiritual part keeps you in balance. It is the part that separates you from animals, and puts you in tune with the Creator to have and live a good life.

"Always remember these three things: first, physically you are in superior shape; second, mentally you are very intelligent. But third, spirituality is the most important, it's the one that gives you mind over matter. All three must be in balance. Spirituality will give you the power to say no to drugs, smoking and other destructive things that will ruin your life.

"This test will give you this balance. Delilah brought down Samson, the world's strongest man. Bathsheba got to King David and several ladies have even got to me. And you have another gift that no money, not even gold, can buy. That is me, and the training I have given you, and still am giving you." He lets out a big sigh as he looks from me to Fox and back at me again, his lips set in a straight line.

"Now, do I keep talking, or do I have your word?"

We drop our heads, and, sadly, slowly give our word.

"You can call this your Adam test." Pops smiles, "Whenever you get weak, think of his story. And, oh, yes—there is one more thing. You two must go to Rebecca and ask her forgiveness. And War, you tell her you will never do that again."

"Yes, Pops," we say, and I know I have to do it, but I wonder how.

"You boys don't seem to be in a very good mood, so Fox you can go," Pops says. "Only War in the dojo today for a short workout." Pops picks up his cane just as Jade comes out of the house. He gives it to her and says, "Let the work-out begin."

Pops always says defense is more important than offense, because the idea is to hit and not be hit. Jade has fire in her eyes, and she swings the cane hard and fast. My body contorts as the cane whistles inches from my chin. I am in for one hell of a time. I used to get black and blue marks all over me when I first started, but now my reflexes are so sharp it's almost impossible to hit me. But Jade tries. She jabs, swings and pokes, and then moves into the Dojo, making me back out. Then she drops the cane and attacks me herself, fists flying, and I'm dodging and blocking.

"Why are you doing this?" I ask.

"You and...Rebecca, that Black hussy."

Pops and Fox have left. I guess it's up to us to deal with this. So I grab her and pull her to the ground.

"You and I are not boyfriend and girlfriend, so why are you so mad at me?"

"I see the way you look at me. You can't keep your eyes off me," she says. "I look at you the same way. I peep out the window when you work out and my body wants you. I thought you liked me. But you are sleeping with Rebecca."

"Okay. If you will be my girlfriend, I won't sleep with her, or anybody else in Tryon. On my word of honor, I will only be with you. You're right. I can't keep my eyes off you. I even see you in my dreams at night, and I am truly in love with you."

She turns, and our eyes meet for a long time. Her eyes are like looking into a pool of beauty. She kisses me and says, "Goodnight boyfriend," then gets up and hurries into the house.

This is different from the Black girl. It makes me feel warm inside—so peaceful, joyous, like opening up your toys at Christmas. But then the real truth hits me. This really is like having Christmas, but not being able to open your presents. My thing is as hard as Japanese arithmetic, but my promise to Pops, my Adam test, means no present for me. And like Fox, I have a tear in my eye. I know I must keep the vow to Pops, but it is not going to be easy. I walk home happy and sad at the same time—happy because I have Jade as my girlfriend, but sad because I'm not gonna be getting any presents.

10
War Dogs

I want to slow down; the summer is going too fast. I have only a couple of months left before I go north. Fox and I have been spending a lot of time on the outdoor basketball court, but today we go back to Heaven with Sun and Head. As we walk the banks of the river we find a Muscadine vine, a form of a wild grape that has big vines that grow in trees. We cut one and make a swing over the water. We swing out, turn loose and fall several feet into the river.

Head swings out, turns loose and does a perfect swan dive into the water. We all try it, but no one can do it but him. It did Head a world of good to do something none of us could, and we had to hear him calling us chumps all day. This only makes Heaven a more special place. It's a lot of fun.

A few weeks ago we made a pact. We broke an arrow like Cochise, the Apache Indian Chief in *Broken Arrow* and swore revenge on the White man for taking our clothes. But we've been swimming in Heaven for weeks and no one has come or bothered us. We have fun swimming and swinging out over the water until it's time to go.

On the way up the bank to the road, Sun says, "Look over yonder." We turn and see two tall black and tan dogs coming our way. Quickly Sun, Head, and I set off running for the woods. But Fox doesn't move. I stop and look at him.

"Fox, you lost your mind?" I ask. "You'd better come on.

Those dogs will tear you apart."

He looks at me and says "With a name like War, and all the training we do, you afraid of a little dog?"

I am definitely afraid, but don't want to look like a coward, or leave my friend alone. So I walk up beside Fox and watch as the two dogs set upon us.

"You damn fools!" Sun hollers from the woods. "That karate shit gonna get y'all ate up! Fools at least pick up a rock or stick or something to hit them war dogs with."

The slightly bigger one heads straight for Fox and the other one comes at me fast. Now I know what Pops means when he says, "Stay centered, like in the eye of a storm. In the center of a hurricane you are safe, but outside is destruction." So I don't panic. Instead I concentrate my forces on the center of one dog's mouth. He leaps for my throat, and I twist to the side like a great matador in the bull ring, punching him in his side as he goes by.

The big dog hits the ground and starts spinning around in circles from the pain in his side. All of a sudden he takes off and runs back the way he came. I look around to see how Fox has done, and can't believe my eyes. The big dog is standing in front of him and they're staring at each other.

"Down," he says. The dog lies down and Fox walks over, pats him on the head, and says, "Come." The dog follows him. We walk up the road with him leading that dog, and I can't believe my eyes. How could Fox do such a thing? Now I know I have to learn more about this meditation, this inner strength Pops always talks about.

When we get into the woods Sun and Head wait up in a tree.

"Where you get that war dog?" Sun hollers.

"Come on down out of the tree. He won't bite you," Fox says.

"I ain't coming nowhere with that war dog down there. I bet you he's been trained to kill Black folks, and black as I am, I ain't getting nowhere near that dog," Sun says.

Fox can't talk them out of the tree, so we head home with Fox's new buddy. The next morning we run with the big dog right beside us. It's fun. When we finish, Pops comes out and rubs the dog down.

"What's his name?" Pops asks.

"Don't know yet. He's so black. Maybe I'll call him 'Midnight,'" Fox says.

"That's a dumb name for a Doberman. It sounds more like a horse." I say. Then I have an idea, "Hey! It just came to me! Why don't you name him Doby after Larry Doby, the first Negro to play in the American League?"

"Doby. That's a cool name," Pops says. "But why can't we call him Doby 'cause he's a Doberman? But, if you want to think it's after Larry Doby, that's on you. However, you just named him! Come on, Doby. Here, Doby!" Pops calls.

"Looks like you just brought Pops home a dog. I think Doby is his now," I say. "He seems to really love that dog."

Fox and I leave and head uptown to get some ice cream. We always run with our shirts off and leave them off while walking down the main street. Two old White ladies look at our bodies so hard they almost walk into us.

"Excuse us," one of the old ladies says. "We saw you coming up the street and wondered what kind of people you good looking boys were, with your long black hair and sexy pretty bodies. Y'all ain't no Negroes are you?"

"I'm just an old country boy, ma'am," Fox jokingly says,

"with a tan and on my way to the movies to see a good shoot 'em up, and get a haircut after the movies. That's all, Mrs."

"Well, don't get it cut, because it looks so nice and would be a shame to cut it. If we were a little younger, you boys would be in trouble." They both laugh as they walk away. The Sheriff happens to be driving by. He slams on his brakes, stops his truck and gets out. Rushing up to us he says, "I bin lookin' for you two funny-lookin' Negroes."

"I ain't no Negro. I'm Asian," Fox says.

"Shut up boy, you sho' ain't White. I say you Colored, so shut up and stay in your place, 'fore I have to put you there," the Sheriff says. "Besides, somebody's been lying to me. First they tell me y'all beat up all those boys in the movies. Now I'm told you stole my buddy's champion Doberman Pinscher.

"I know that damn dog. He is one mean son of a bitch. Ain't nobody can get near him." He gestures toward his truck. "I have one of my blue tick hounds in the back of my pickup, one day, visiting my buddy, when that damn dog jumps in the back of the truck and kills my hound dead. He then had the nerve to growl at me when I came out with my pistol drawn. I was gonna shoot that son-of-a-bitch till my buddy grabbed my arm and talked me out of it. And now they tell me y'all just walked off with him. Somebody is lyin' to me."

He spits tobacco juice to his left and hooks his thumbs into his front pants pockets.

"And now you boys walk 'round here wit' your shirts off like y'all is White. You boys even forget to move off the sidewalk when you see White ladies comin' down the street. Don't you know I can put you in jail for that? Shamin' White ladies with your chest all out like that, you boys makin' me look bad. In the old days, your ass would've been tied up and horse whipped. But now, with all this marchin' and sit-in bullshit, even got some White people from up north marchin' and carrying on. They need to keep their asses up north where they belong and stay out of Southern Business. They make you people think you can act and do just about as you please," he says.

"But I'm gonna give you a chance to make me fergit all those things and see if what they say about you is true." He looks us up and down with suspicion.

"You boys meet me over at the White school football field in half an hour."

"But Mister Sheriff, we're on our way to the movie," Fox says.

"Let me put it to you this way. If you ain't over to that field in half an hour, your ass is grass and I am the lawn-mower."

He walks away and gets in his pickup and takes off like a bat out of hell.

We're looking at each other.

"I wonder what this crazy ass Sheriff could possibly want?" Fox says, "Did you smell that whiskey on his breath? That fool is drunk as a skunk. It must be his day off. His old lady must not have given him any! He's as ornery as a snake!"

"Drunk, ornery or not, I guess the movie is out. We'd better head over to the field. We don't need that racist Sheriff on our backs," I say.

When we get to the football field we see the Sheriff and several other men there. One well-built young man is off to the side, shadow boxing.

11

International Karate Championship

I'm gonna git right to the point," the Sheriff says, "The first International Karate Championships for boys eighteen and under is gonna be in South Carolina next week, part of a big Fourth of July celebration.

"The boys and I have a heap of money bet on our boy to win. Even put up my best blue tick hound against some ol' boy's best Redbone Hound on our North Carolina boy to win. Losing the money would hurt my pocket book, but losing my blue tick will break my heart. Now International means anybody 'cep' a Colored boy. You light-skin boy might pass for an Indian, or maybe a Mexican, but they don't let them in either."

All the men bust out laughing. The Sheriff looks Fox in the eye.

"You, Asian Negro, you can be a Jap or a Chinaman. I can pull a few strings and get you in."

The Sheriff goes on. "I told my good buddies here about y'all beatin' up those boys in the movies, and that one of you might beat old Jumbo over there. When they finally stopped laughin', they ask me to come and find you boys, so old Jumbo can get a work-out and some practice kickin' ass before he heads south. In case you boys don't know it, he's the North Carolina champ and never been beat. Does one of you boys want to give it a try?"

"What do we get after I kick this big chump's behind?" Fox asks the Sheriff. All the men have a good laugh at Fox.

"You can keep the dog. Besides, my buddy says he don't want no dog that just up and walks off with a bunch of Niggers anyway. That's all well and good, but the best thing is y'all will be my boys. And ain't nobody messes wit' the Sheriff's boys."

One of the other men speaks up.

"By God if you win, I'll give you ice cream sodas free on Saturday on your way to the movies, but a snowball covered with gas has a better chance in hell than you do of kicking Jumbo's ass." He slaps his leg, laughing like he's lost his mind.

Jumbo steps up and says, "This is crazy. No raggedy-tail, untrained teenager can even give me a good fight. Y'all wastin' my time and 'bout to get these young boys hurt."

"Sheriff, next year we play basketball in the White gym. After I kick Jumbo's ass, can the boys and I start playing there over the summer?" Fox says.

"Hell yes! My boys get what they want. So you and the Colored boys can use it right away. Besides, Tryon will have a helluva basketball team if we can put some niggers on it next year. Boy you sho' do talk a good game. You sound like you really believe you might win this fight. Now enough of this chatter. You two face off, and let's fight."

"Okay, Sheriff. If I kick Jumbo's ass, will you please stop calling me a Negro, Colored, or Nigger, because I am Asian!"

"Better than that, boy! I'll call you by your name. Now enough talk. Let's get this show on the road!"

Jumbo and Fox go at it. The White boy fakes a punch and tries to dive low and take Fox off his feet. That is a big mistake. As Fox jumps up, the boy goes under and Fox turns in

the air, landing on the White boy's back. He grabs him under
the chin and pulls the boy's head back. The fight is over in
less than ten seconds.

Then they go at it again, because the White guys think it's
luck. Jumbo warns Fox this time he's going to hurt him, then
circles slowly, throws several punches and kicks. Fox ducks
and blocks all of them. Fox seems to get tired of this and,
like lightning, he snap-kicks the boy in the solar plexus.
Jumbo falls over and rolls on the ground. The fight is over
just that quick! I can't help but wonder just what kind of
champion this Jumbo boy is.

It looks as though I'm about to find out, because the
Sheriff says, "By Gawd, I ain't nevah seen nothin' like this
in my life. That Jap…Chinaman…Mongolian…whatever he
is, is one bad son-of-a-gun." He turns to me.

"Now you, you red Negro, what they call you?"

"War, Mr. Sheriff, short for Warrior."

"What kind of a name is that for a Colored? Well, we
gonna see if you live up to yo' name, boy. Jumbo, you sit
there and git yourself together, so you can whip this red
Nigger ass, you hear?"

"Sheriff, don't call me a Nigger! I have some of Daniel
Boone's blood in me, so, call me White!"

"You two boys have pissed me off with this I ain't no
Nigger shit! Jumbo you better whip this young Nigger ass—
and whip it good."

I take a good look at Jumbo. He's a senior in high school
and much bigger and stronger than I am. Flustered and mad
as hell about losing to Fox, he is ready to take it out on me.
I have never been in a real karate fight and feel like a man
about to die, with his life passing before him.

I steal a quick look at Fox and the strangest thing happens. Pops comes to my mind. I know Sun and Pops think the Asians are a superior race, for they think they are smarter, eat better, and have a better lifestyle. I'm not even sure what I am, but if it's Indian, I know the Cherokee feel they're superior, for they have lived off the land. Grandma always tells me the "White man goes into his church to learn about God, while the Cherokee goes into his tepee to live with God." If I'm a Negro, then I know they feel they are faster like Jesse Owens and stronger like Joe Louis, and well hung. So how could the White part of me be superior? The White man doesn't think he's superior, he just knows it. He has all the good jobs, money, power, the guns and owns the whole country, and everyone else is a second-class citizen.

But now none of that matters, for it's man on man, me against this big, flustered, angry karate expert. And he is ready. We bow to each other, and it's on! We battle for some time, and his strength is taking its toll on me. He is much better than I thought. Fox took him so easy, and he is kicking my butt! He punches me and I feel my strength leaving. Pain! I'm going down. He leans over me as I fall. At that moment I remember Pops holding up the board for us to break. I kick up, catching him under his chin. As I hit the ground, I turn slowly, painfully, to look over at Jumbo. He is out, flat on his back. I manage to get to my feet, and get in my stance and let out a karate yell like I am not hurting.

The Sheriff hollers, "By Gawd! Ever' thing they say 'bout you boys is true! Y'all some bad Negroes! An' now you my Negroes and y'all can use the gym any time. So go home, Colored boy! Excuse me. I mean 'Asian boy' and tell your grandpa that next week we goin' to South Carolina to whip some folks down there! And that's all there is to that!"

"Sorry, Sheriff," Fox says, "but I don't think my Grandpa will let me go. And my name is Fox, not Asian boy."

The Sheriff laughs.

"Okay, Fox. I hear tell yo' old grandpa is brewin' up stuff in the back yard that's against the law, if you know what I mean, and raising some funny tobacco. Now this is my town, Fox, and I know everythin' going on. I kind of look the other way, 'cause the mayor gits him a little taste now and then, and an old girlfriend of mine gets real frisky after one or two drinks of that brew. Now I can stomach the mayor fallin' out with me, but I don't want to lose my good thing, if you know what I mean? So you see I sho' would hate to call the revenue in on the old boy to check him out. But if we're going to South Carolina, the Sheriff will be happy and don't know nothin'. So you tell him to have you ready next week, you heah?"

On the walk to Fox's house every part of my body hurts from the fight. As we enter his house, Pops comes down and gives me a shot of hot sake and puts me in this steam room. I begin to think maybe the Asians really are superior. After several minutes he takes me into a room with a big bathtub in the center. We all take off our clothes and get in the bath. Pops' body is still lean, and his stomach is flat, even though he's real old. The bath has minerals in it. It's very relaxing, but the best is yet to come.

Jade comes in holding a long, colorful robe, waving for me to get out of the water. When I step up she wraps the robe around me, leads me to a table and tells me to lie down on my stomach. I don't think she's going to give me some, but the thought does cross my mind. I have no idea what's up.

She places a large white towel over my butt and sprinkles some warm oil on my back. She lights some incense that smells like flowers from the Orient. Soft Asian music plays as her fingers stroke, pull and push, soothing and stimulating my aching muscles. She takes her long black hair and lets it barely tickle me as it falls across my body like a magic wand. This is my first massage, and it's almost as good as my first time I tried to get some. My hurt slowly fades away as I drift off into an almost hypnotic sleep.

I, who am of three races, Indian, Black, and White, finally know there is no such thing as a superior race, or any races at all, only different and superior kinds of people. Although the blood of three races runs through my veins I can only be one race, and that one is human.

The Asians may be superior in stimulating the body and martial arts, and I'm learning that from them. But more important, I am learning the true meaning of friendship. I give thanks to the Creator for my adopted family. And although I will never be Asian, I already am, in spirit.

12
Chitlins

The *Tryon Daily Bulletin* is the world's smallest daily newspaper. Fox and I have been carrying them for several years. It's how I get my movie money, Baby Ruth candy bars and soda money. We meet at the Bulletin office uptown, and he goes west and I go east. But we both have White and Colored customers. Sometimes it's hard, because after we finish our routes we still have to do the run. The Bulletin goes for ten cents a week and we keep eight along with tips and selling a few on the side. We both have about seventy customers; so, it's worth it.

A couple days before Fox is going south to fight, after finishing my route, me and Grandma are sitting on the front porch. She has already told me there is no way I am going south. I hand her an RC Cola, her favorite soda, trying to soften her up to let me go.

"Grandma please let me go see Fox fight," I beg.

"Hell, no," she says, the first and only time I ever heard her cuss. "I hear tell you bin foolin' roun' with that little fast Black gal down in the hollow. Done told you 'bout them Black girls. When she puts a hex on you don't come a runnin' to me. Beside, you still too young to fool around with girls. You better let that thing finish growing, so you can do some woman some good some day. And no, you ain't goin' south, so get it out of your mind."

I know what she's really mad about is that my uncle has got the Black girl he's going with pregnant, and I know I have to suffer because of him.

About that time I see him coming up to the house, looking real bad. He doesn't say anything; he just opens the little door that goes under the house, where we keep our push lawnmower and garden tools and stuff.

"Lord, if you let me live I'll never drink again," he says moaning and throwing up under the house. The dirt is real loose under there, and he must've laid down, rolled around in and got nasty stuff all over him.

Uncle tells me later that he and Candy are leaving for the army tomorrow, going to Vietnam. He goes by his Black girlfriend's house where she tries to screw him to death. She then fixes him lots of the chitlins he loves so much with lots of Red Devil hot sauce.

The big boys give him a going-away party, and he drinks lots of corn whiskey. The combination of eating chitlins and drinking white lightning messes up his stomach so bad stuff is coming out of both ends. Uncle says he feels like he was dying.

"I told you that Black gal gonna put a spell on you!" Grandma shouts. "Bring your drunk ass out from under the porch and I mean right now. I need to take a switch and beat yo' ass, but you grown now and if you ain't got no common sense by now, shame on you."

My uncle stinks as he comes out from under the house, and smells like he has gone to the bathroom all over himself.

"Take off all your stinking clothes, 'cept your underwear." Grandma yells. Then she throws his clothes in an old black cast iron tub with some homemade lye soap.

She sprays them with the hose, and then sprays Uncle down from head to toe.

I'm not sure what chitlins are, so I ask Grandma.

"Boy, don't play dumb," she says. "You live in the south! Just because we never cook those smelly things, you damn well know they're hog intestines."

I know that, but just can't believe anyone would eat hog intestines! Thanks to Uncle, to this day I can't stand to smell or eat chitlins.

Me and Fox tell Pops about Charleston and, to our surprise, he likes the idea. The next few days the training gets much longer and harder as Pops makes us do defense drills first, then offense drills, and then both together. About all we do is carry our Bulletins, eat, and drill some more. I've never seen Fox so uptight. I'm sure he's worried about the tournament. We throw punches for one hour straight, until Pops finally says to stop.

Fox walks over and picks up a board and pitches it to Pops.

"Hold it up!" he says.

He walks over to Pops, closes his eyes, and meditates for a few seconds. Fox takes a deep breath, rocks back and forth, and leaps up, kicking. His foot shatters the board. Even before he hits the ground, he's screaming, "I did it! I did it! I broke the board."

He rushes over, hugging me and whispering in my ear.

"They think I'm happy because I broke the board and I am, but the real reason is now I can get some next year at seventeen."

Jade comes out of the house, and we are all yelling and screaming.

"He did it. He did it. Fox broke the board." But I know he's happier his Adam test is over next year.

Not to be outdone, I pitch Pops a board and leap up and kick it. It doesn't break, but I'm close. After that, the training goes smoother. Fox is relaxed and sharp, blocking and punching. He has broken the board. He's ready for Charleston.

13
Grandma

Grandma and I sit in the swing on the porch that afternoon, and I try to sweet-talk her into letting me go to Charleston.

"Boy you gettin' on my last nerves and don't keep askin' 'cause you ain't goin' nowhere," she says.

I can't understand how she can be so mean. I have to find a way. I have to see Fox fight. But I have run out of ideas. Fox and the Sheriff are leaving tomorrow, so I'm just sitting here feeling sad and hurting.

"Grandma, I'll paint the house, clean up the back yard—anything! Just let me go see my buddy fight. Besides, I have never been to a big city like Charleston. It will give me some idea what it will be like up North."

"Boy, you know that hedge bush out back has some mighty nice switches on it, since I haven't had to whip you or that Black-girl loving son of mine lately. I don't whip you any more 'cause you are fourteen and old enough to have some sense. If you keep messing with me, I'm goin' to light your behind up! Now stop your whinin', Boy! You ain't going nowhere till you go up North to school in the fall!"

"Okay, Grandma, but if you change your mind, let me know."

About that time I see Pops walking up the path to our house with a small Mason jar of sake in his hand. He walks right by me and just looks at me. With slight motions of his head he gives me a signal to leave. I do, and then double back close enough to see Grandma sitting in the swing, talking, laughing and sipping from the Mason jar. I leave and go to the basketball court, with some hope I may go south yet.

When I get back home it's almost dark, and I see Pops walking down the pathway with a sweet potato pie in his hand and a smile on his face. As I walk up on the porch, Grandma sits in the swing humming. Her dress is slightly wrinkled, and the Mason jar is empty. I'm thinking maybe they have a thing going, but she is in her fifties and Pops is older than that. But it sure looks like they have done it!

She looks at me and says, "You been such a good boy, if you go cut up that wood in the back yard, I might let you go south tomorrow."

Now I know Pops must've got some and he must've done a good job. And I know I'm going south, but I'm a wood chopping fool any way.

14
Charleston

I feel like a little child at Christmas, I'm so excited to be going to a big city to see Fox fight. We want Pops to go with us, but he says no, because it will be a good learning experience for us alone.

He tells Sun to use the name Woo, to honor his favorite karate teacher's name in Asia.

"Be brave and make me and the name Woo proud." Giving us a big hug before we get in the Sheriff's car, Pops waves at us as we drive away. Fox and I sit in the back and the Sheriff, the Mayor and—of all people—the redneck who took our clothes while we were swimming, in the front. It turns out he owns all the land around Heaven.

This is the White power structure in Tryon. A bumper sticker on the Sheriff's big Chevy reads 'Lee surrendered, not me.' Plus, we are going to Charleston, the Mecca of the South. We are knee deep in White folks and a little uneasy.

Several hours later we arrive in the heart of the South. Segregation seems much worse here than in Tryon. In Tryon we see small signs in a few windows saying "No Colored," but here it's big signs that say "No Colored" or "Colored to the Rear" or just plain "We Don't Serve Colored." We're in Charleston.

I see my first palm tree. It's beautiful. The city, houses, streets, everything seems so big after always living in Tryon. We ride along admiring the city when Redneck hollers "Barbecue ribs! Pull over. Let's eat."

We park, and without thinking walk with them into the front door of this Southern style café. The aroma from the BBQ makes my mouth water. It's as if we commit an unforgivable sin, when a pot-bellied-bib-overall-wearing man stands up yelling at the top of his voice.

"I know you niggers ain't from around here! The nerve of you to bring your Black ass in here! We ain't gonna have none of that sit-in bullshit that King fellow started down there in Birmingham. Making them Niggers think they near 'bout good as White folks. You better take your Nigger ass round back where you belong."

Fox, pumped up as he is for the tournament, without thinking, says, "I ain't no Nigger and I ain't Black! I am Asian, and near 'bout to kick your stinking White trash ass till you turn black."

For a moment, the pot-bellied man stands mesmerized in shock, not believing Fox has the nerve to talk to him like that. Several of his buddies stand up, and I stand beside Fox ready to battle.

"Don't just stand there. You're so bad. Come and kick us out," Fox says.

"Easy fellows," the Sheriff shows his badge, while looking at the pot-bellied man. "Don't worry. I'm taking these two uppity boys out to the woodshed after lunch to make sure they know how to talk to White folks. Know what I mean?"

The pot-bellied man, points his finger at Fox, "Somebody better straighten them Nigger boys out," he says. "Teach them some manners, and put them in their place 'fore we have to."

Then the Sheriff slaps Fox—not very hard, but he makes

it look worse than it is.

"You betta listen. It's the tournament, or jail! Take your choice," he says. "Now take your butts round back and eat your lunch."

So we do. We walk around the back and see several old Colored men eating and playing cards and checkers as we get our food.

One of the old men stands up and says, "You boys ain't from 'round heah! Where you from?"

We tell them, from Tryon and that Fox is in the karate tournament. They burst out laughing, "They don't let none of us in there."

Then one of the old men pointing at Fox says, "He ain't one of us. He's a foreigner."

Another asks Fox, "What foreign country you from, boy?"

"I was born in Asia, but raised and live on the Colored side of town. I get treated like shit, same as you, so guess I'm Colored too. I want y'all to bet on me to win the tournament."

The old men laugh so hard they almost fall out of their seats.

"Y'all must not know it, but big Jesse is fighting in that tournament. He is a known Klan member, hates anything Colored, so boy, you better take out some insurance!"

Fox, still steaming from the pot-belly man calling him a Nigger, says, "Come on War, let's show these gentlemen what karate is all about." Then we do some punches and kicks, and put on one hell of an exhibition. When we finish, we look around. One of the old men has knocked over the checker board; another has dropped his corn cob pipe.

"Boy, you sho' is fast," one says. "They call me Hawk, and we gonna pray for you and put our money on you 'cause we hate that son of a bitch Jesse, walkin' around here like his stuff don't stink. I used to play ball in the Negro Baseball league. You boys know 'bout Satchel Page, our greatest pitcher with his do-drop-in curve ball and Josh Gibson, our greatest hitter. They say once he hit a ball out of Yankee Stadium. Boy, you as fast as one of our players we called 'Cool Papa Bell' who was so fast he could cut out the lights and be in bed before it got dark. So use your speed and go put Jesse's light out, young cool Papa."

The old men have Fox feeling much better now, so we go around front to meet the Sheriff. He says, "Let's take a walking tour." He and Redneck go their way and Fox and I go ours. We walk by this swinging blues club loaded with people—all White but the blues band is Colored. A young Negro is shining shoes in front of this hotel. One older, very refined looking Colored man, staggers trying to carry a young couple's bags while the young White man pays him no mind.

15

Slaves Market Place

We come to the market place. They must have forgotten to put "Slave" in front of it, for it really is a museum where they used to sell slaves.

"Let's walk up the steps," I say to Fox.

At the top, I turn around. Looking out over the crowd, this eerie feeling comes over me. I am back in 1864, one hundred years ago.

I am a slave and this old man who looks like Colonel Sanders from Kentucky Fried Chicken, holds his hand up saying, "I bid one thousand dollars for that young light Nigger. I can train him to fetch my shoes, run my bath water. I can get twenty or thirty good years out of him, make him my number one house boy."

For a moment I feel the pain of my ancestors, to stand up here like an animal, less than human. To be sold like a mule is beyond my understanding. To do all the work, make some White man rich and then have him show you the place in the Bible where he says if you serve him as your master you'll get your reward in Heaven. Yet call himself a Christian, even has the nerve to think a slave would believe that crap.

Fox nudges me, asking about the chains that still lie on the floor; I explain they were used to hold slaves until they were sold.

Fox can't believe men could be so mean and savage. Then he closes his eyes and takes deep breaths and makes strange low noises. He falls into a trance and flexes his muscles and whispers in a strange voice, "The ghosts of Black slave warriors are entering my body. They tell me to whip some Cracker's ass. This will help them rest in peace, and I must win the tournament for them."

Still in a trance, he walks down into the crowd right up to this fine blonde young lady. He whispers something into her ear and she comes up the steps and hugs me. Somehow Fox gets this pretty blonde lady to come up and hug me, right here in the Mecca of the segregated South!

"I wonder how many old Southerners are turning over in their graves with me hugging you like this." The blonde lady whispers in my ear. "And look at the faces of the people in the crowd. They ain't too happy about it either."

Just about this time the Sheriff comes up.

"Hey, you boys get out from up there!" he hollers.

Fox, still in a trance-like state, doesn't move.

Redneck laughs and says, "How you gonna win with that Asian Nigger? He's out in space!"

That word awakens Fox, and he says in a clowning way, "Yes good boss man, Sheriff, I's comin', don't beat me Massa Sheriff, I's be a good Asian Nigger. Watch me coon fer yo' boss." He whistles and does a little soft shoe dance.

"That boy is sick," Redneck grimaces. "And we bet all that money and your best blue tick on him. Maybe we the one that's crazy."

"He might be a little strange," the Sheriff says, "but he can kick ass. Let's go check into our hotel."

We walk up to this beautiful grand old hotel, like something out of the movie *Gone with the Wind*. We wait outside while the Sheriff goes in. Shortly he comes back.

"You boys know can't no Negroes stay in no hotel around

here," he says, "and the owner wants me to send you boys, cross the railroad tracks to stay with some Nigger woman that takes in Colored. I'm doing you boys a favor, he's gonna let you sleep round back."

A Black maid comes out with some blankets and pillows. She asks us to follow her, leading us around back to a little shanty-like cabin.

"You sleep here," she says.

As we enter, the true meaning of segregation hits me. There are a couple of pails for going to the toilet, a few beds with well-worn springs for mattresses and a kerosene lamp for light. This is barely a step up from a slave's cabin.

"I wonder if this is 1964 or 1864," I say to Fox.

"To hell with this! I ain't fighting! That damn Sheriff is just using us. I used to think Colored people complained too much, always bitching about this or that. I had no idea all the bullshit you have to put up with. I see now being Colored is pure hell and I'm in the same boat. Screw the White man! He ain't going to use me," Fox says, as he pees in the pail.

"So what? White folks been using us for years, but we use them too. Just think, if you win, Jolene might give you some! And remember, we get free ice cream every Saturday. Besides you get to beat up White boys without going to jail. Also, tell the Sheriff you want some money to fight. Don't let that Cracker use you for nothing."

"Okay. Don't sound bad, besides I don't want those slave warriors hunting me. It's been a long day. Let's get some shut-eye so I can kick some Cracker butt tomorrow," Fox says, as he stretches out on the well-used mattress. In no time he's fast asleep.

16
Fight Day

In the morning the Sheriff opens the door yelling, "By God, it smells like an outhouse in here."

He pitches in some GI (long white karate training pants and a loose fitting jacket) for us to wear in the tournament.

"Hurry up, wash your asses so we can get breakfast."

Dressed in our GI we feel like true karate warriors. We ride across some railroad tracks into another world called Colored Town. The houses are old and raggedy, like most of the houses are on the Colored sides of towns in the South. On the way, the Sheriff picks up his friend Monroe who lives in Charleston. He takes us to this great little Colored restaurant, where we have pancakes, country ham, grits and eggs. Funny, they can eat in our restaurants, but we can't eat in theirs.

On our way back to the tournament, Redneck turns to me and says, "Boy, I want you to learn to say and spell Reggio, 'cause that's your new name. You are Italian, and can't speak no English, none at all. You have made a vow of silence, so shut up and let me do all your talking from now on. I don't want you to talk to nobody, understand?"

I say okay. I have no idea what he's talking about, but I know to keep my mouth shut. I like the idea. With my long black hair, maybe I could pass for Italian; sit in the White-only section and watch Fox fight. Redneck is smarter than I thought.

We enter the arena and a strange feeling comes over me,

one like I have never had before. How could I pass for someone from another country who can't even speak English and be welcomed, yet live in America and can't go where this non-American Italian who had never even been in America before can go?

I don't follow the Civil Rights movement much in Tryon. I know about the little girls blown up in the church in Birmingham, the sit-ins, King's marching and going to jail. But the Southern radio and newspapers play it down.

Besides, in Tryon we have our own baseball team, night clubs, schools and churches and live well. At least I think we do until I come here and really understand the meaning of Sun's favorite saying, "Ignorance is bliss." He always talks about the White man keeping us ignorant so we think we are happy. How, if the slaves were caught trying to learn to read or write, they were hung, and it ain't too much better now.

In the arena the only thing black or brown in there, besides us, are the belts all the young White boys are wearing around the waist on their GI. I haven't seen this much white since the last snow.

They take us over to sign Fox in, and the Sheriff winks at the man, slides him some money

"This is Woo," he says. "He's a black belt from the House of Tryon. He's fighting in the open competition. This other one's my cousin from Italy. His name is Reggio and he can't speak a lick of English. He's a Sicilian. And you know what they say about them, 'Dumb as hell and almost as dark as Niggers.' Put him in the novice's competition. Let him get his foreign ass kicked."

They both laugh, and the Sheriff gives the man the entry money for Woo and Reggio.

I don't know what to do. I had no idea I'd be fighting, but I'm scared to say anything. Fox is glad.

"Let's win both belts," he says.

The idea doesn't seem so bad anymore.

Walking around admiring this magnificent arena with this huge crowd of White folks my eyes can't believe what I see. In a small roped off section a sign says 'COLORED SECTION D.' Even more surprising, the old men who played checkers behind the café are there, and the one named Hawk is holding up a sign saying "GO COOL PAPA."

Fox walks up and waves at Hawk.

"Let's win it for Hawk, the Black Slave Warriors, Pops, and Cool Papa Bell," he whispers.

"Sounds like a great idea," I say.

Now I am getting excited. All at once the arena explodes in a loud roar as the two South Carolina fighters come in. The one with the black belt has muscles on muscles.

"There's Jesse the Champ," someone in the crowd says. "They say he was in the Seals, got in a fight with some soldiers and put several of them in the hospital, so he got kicked out of the Seals."

Another in the crowd says, "Butch is fighting in novices. We all know he's good enough to have his black belt."

Someone else says, "Ain't no living' ass gonna stand a chance against our South Carolina boys."

Redneck taps us on the shoulder, and takes us over to the judge. He explains the rules, which are not many.

"No eye poking, biting, head butts, or striking in the throat or in the two little brothers. That's 'bout it."

I don't know what black or brown belts mean, just that

there are twenty in my lineup and only sixteen in Fox's. I have to win four fights today, and Fox only three, for us to fight in the championships tomorrow. This is when I get real scared. But Fox has a smile on his face, so I relax. We're lucky to see a couple of fights before ours. Butch, my opponent, is one of them. Fox says he has a very bad weakness.

"Please tell me," I beg.

"If I do, you will be looking for it instead of fighting. You must figure it out yourself," Fox says.

Butch wins easily, and the only weakness I see is his opponent hitting the deck. He looks real sharp to me.

I hear the name Reggio, and for a moment don't realize they are calling me. As I step in the ring, I see that my opponent is more nervous than I am. He has good technique, but he's slower than molasses in January, and I win on points. As I wait for my next fight, I see Jesse kick his opponent clear out of the ring! I'm glad I don't have to fight him. Fox is poetry in motion, but has to struggle to out-point his opponent.

My next two fights are hell, but I win one on points and the other with a K.O. Fox also wins his match. We are both dog-tired as we break to get something to eat and rest before we come back for the semi-finals. I think we're both about ready to quit. We eat something light, and Fox opens the letter Pops gave him with instructions to open it at a time like this.

17

Nirvana

In the great religion of Buddhism," Fox reads, " Nirvana is a state of mind in which you live for the present and put all your energy and thought into the now, not into the past or the future. Operate where you are, and focus on the moment. Remember, you were taught by Pops. Now make me and the name Woo proud."

This is the kick-start we need. We go back into the arena and win, and are in the championship finals tomorrow. It's not a surprise to see Jesse and his brown-belt buddy, Butch, also in the finals. It's going to be a hell of a match tomorrow.

It's late as we leave the arena, but there is still a lot of daylight left. We want to walk slowly around the town and sightsee a little before we go to the barn to rest our tired bodies.

The Sheriff and his friend Monroe pull up in this new shiny red four-speed-on-the-floor Pontiac GTO, and tells us to get in. I think something is wrong with his motor because it has a loping sound like it is going to cut off. No sooner do we get in our seats, when Monroe floors that GTO and every time he shifts gears it throws us back in our seats and the Sheriff lets out this rebel yell "Yew how." This is one hell of a fast car and I have the ride of my life. We ride a few miles until we come to a big Southern mansion. At first I think it is a hotel; it is so big.

"Get out. Welcome to my little neck of the woods," says

Monroe.

Fox and I walk slowly, not knowing what to expect, but it sure looks like having won a few fights means we're going from the barn to a big mansion.

"Come on in," Monroe says and introduces us to his wife and a few friends. He brags about us being in the finals tomorrow.

"You boys must be dead tired. Come on, let me show you to your room," Monroe's wife says.

She gives us some soap, towels, and nice soft white robes then takes us to the biggest bedroom I ever saw. It has two beds and a bathroom the size of a small house.

"Wash up and I'll call you down for supper in a while." She shuts the door.

I know we are the first and only Colored to be in here other than to house clean. We take our first shower, and boy, does it feel good!

Afterwards we even get in the bathtub, and make lots of bubbles in the hot water. The aches and pain from the fights just melt away. Now I know how my White ancestors really lived, and I like it. We are so relaxed after the bath we fall asleep.

Some time later we hear a knock on the door.

"Come and get it."

We dress and go down to one of the best dinners I've ever tasted. We sit at this big table, with everything from greens and black-eyed peas to pork chops, and the best fried chicken (next to Grandma's) I have ever eaten.

"This food is so good the cook has to be Black!" Fox whispers to me.

We eat and eat, and as we are just about to finish,

Monroe's wife brings out some peach cobbler.

"These peaches came fresh off the tree. You can't get store-bought fruit to make a pie like this. Hope you boys enjoyed my cooking. I just love to cook. Can't you tell by how fat old hubby is?" Monroe's wife says, pointing at him and laughing as she goes back into the kitchen

"I always believed White folks couldn't cook, but she sure killed that idea," Fox whispers.

We thank her and tell her how really good the food is.

"You boys gonna sleep in the big house tonight," the Sheriff speaks up, " so you can git a good night's sleep and win tomorrow. I tell you what. We gonna give you some incentive to win."

He pulls some money out—a hundred big ones.

"I know y'all got good odds and already won a pocket full of money betting on us." Fox smiles and holds up five fingers.

"Niggah," Redneck yells out, "are you crazy? A young Niggah like you ain't worth no five hunnerd dollahs!"

The owner of the house, Monroe, is laughing his butt off.

"Hey! You drive a hard bargain! If you both win, you deserve it! You will get the five hunnerd apiece," he says.

Fox gets up.

"Thanks," he says, and we head up the stairs to bed.

Now this is true Nirvana. My White ancestors really know how to live and I'm really enjoying this present moment in my White ancestors' world. We hit the big bed, and in no time are fast asleep.

18

Slave Warriors

Some time late in the night the Black slave warriors come to me in a dream about this little White man with a big whip beating all these tall strong Black men. They are crying and begging for mercy. Then the little old White man draws his whip back and it gets caught on a tree limb. He can't get it loose. The tall Black men look up and see he doesn't have the whip anymore. They stand up and look at each other, but they're still scared, because many years of slavery have bred the fear of the White man into them.

One slave stands up and asks, "Are we men or animals?"

Another says "We are sons of brave warriors who used to go into the jungle and fight a lion with a spear. Yet this little White man has all this power over us." They all stand up.

"Let's take our freedom." They move toward the little White man and with his eyes about to pop out of his head, he cries for mercy.

I feel something shaking me, "Wake up! It's time for breakfast," Fox says.

That is some dream. I roll out of bed telling Fox my dream—how the slave warriors are just about to kill the slave master.

"You woke me up at the best part. They were just about to tar and feather him." Fox just laughs.

"Let's eat. You can go back to sleep and finish kicking the old master's ass after breakfast."

We wash fast, and hurry down to breakfast. The aromas

of freshly brewed coffee and bacon greet us as we approach the breakfast table. All the people get up and leave without saying good morning or anything. There is plenty of food—link sausages, grits, eggs, biscuits, and all the good stuff, but no people.

"Everyone was so nice and happy eating with us last night," Fox frowns. "I bet you Redneck reminded them we are Black, or I should say you are and that Black and White don't mix even at the supper table in Charleston."

"Who gives a kitty? With all the food, it's just more for us," I say as I load my plate.

We finish our food and go back to our room to rest until about eleven. Then we go through our kata, our workout of kicks and punches, most of which are called by animal names: Tiger, Snake, Monkey, and so forth. We do it in slow motion to warm up and sharpen our reflexes.

About noon we head for the arena, because I fight at one. As we ride there I look out the window and can't believe how silent and sad the White people look. It's July the third, and this is the big Fourth of July celebration week. With Willie Nelson and Johnny Cash in town, people should be loud, playing music or something. Yet they look like Kennedy has just been shot.

"Do you notice that the Colored people are acting like fools, " Fox says, "blowing car horns, jumping up and down in the streets? Maybe King is running for president or something."

The Sheriff and Redneck are silent in the front seat when the Sheriff turns and hollers in an angry voice, "Shut your loud mouth and think about the fight."

We don't know what, but something bad is bothering the

White folks.

As we pull up to the arena and get out, we see a group of Colored folks off to the left jumping up and down, waving newspapers, singing *Lift Ev'ry Voice and Sing* also known as *The Black National Anthem*. They are dancing in the streets. Several of the old Colored men from behind the café are holding up signs, saying stuff like 'GO COOL PAPA BELL' and 'WOO AND REGGIO KICK BUTT.' But other signs read 'FREE AT LAST' and 'MARTIN LUTHER IS KING.' I know they are surprised we made the finals, but this seems to be carrying it a bit too far. These Black people in Charleston need to get a life getting this carried away over us winning the championship.

"Don't flatter yourself," Fox laughs, saying, "It ain't us they're celebrating. Read the newspapers they're holding up."

I read one of the papers they're waving and see the real reason they're shouting. The reason the White people are quiet at breakfast this morning, the reason why White people in the streets look so sad, while Colored folks blow car horns and dance in the streets. The paper says that President Johnson passed the Civil Rights Act yesterday July 2nd 1964.

I look at Fox.

"This is our new Independence Day, the end of segregation, and the White Southern people's way of life. We were freed as slaves long ago, but only on paper. Now it's law," I say.

We are now true Americans which means an end to White people pissing all over us. This is what the slave warriors were telling me in my dream last night. I found myself jumping up and down yelling, "Free at last, free at last; Thank God almighty we are free at last."

"It's been a very bad day for the White folks," Fox says. "Now let's give them something else to be mad about and win this tournament."

As we enter the arena I feel a surge of pride. Yesterday I entered as an Italian, but today as a free American. No more not being able to stop at a motel to sleep, or going past nice clean White restrooms to a stinky, smelly one with a Colored sign on them, so bad you wonder how our females use them. No more sitting in the balcony of movies like we are lepers or something nasty. Now I am a true, free American.

Inside the arena it's like a hornet nest, people buzzing around in small groups talking about the Act. Because we have our karate gear on, and not dark complexioned we blend in with the crowd. I feel like a chameleon on the wall listening to them talk. It's enlightening to hear what White folks say when they don't know anyone Colored is around. They even talk about killing President Johnson for passing the Civil Rights Act.

"Don't worry about it," one White man says. "It's just an act, it's not a law. We get the right people in office, we can get it removed, and put them Niggers back in their place."

There's a big crowd around my opponent, and I can hear him talking about how he's going to pick fights with a lot of Niggers in school and mess them up, how no Nigger better come near him in school. How he's gonna start with me, by hurting me so bad they have to carry me out on a stretcher.

All of a sudden I want to hurt this guy. Pops taught us not to hate our opponents, but this one is personal. I can't wait for this fight to start to show Butch he ain't any better than anyone else.

Finally, it's time to fight! As I step into the ring, the crowd is hostile, cheering for my opponent. But the only thing I can see is that dear old man in the Dojo swinging that cane at me, or showing me the correct way to throw a punch and be ready to find my opponent's weakness. I remember the last thing he said as we left Tryon.

"If your opponent is quick, he is dangerous, but if he is patient, watch out!"

So, as much as I want to start fast, I remember patience.

As we come together my opponent throws several punches and catches me with a side-kick to my stomach. It hurts really bad, and the crowd roars. This awakens me to the fact this is no sport, but a fight, and Butch is trying to hurt me. The round ends and I stagger back to my corner.

"Come on, War, you can't let Pops and Hawk down." Fox says, with a worried look. "Get yourself together."

"Relax," I tell him. "My patience has paid off. I found his weakness and will take him out this round."

As we come together, Butch throws punches like a wild man, and kicks at my face. That is his weakness. He holds his leg up a split second too long. He kicks with his right leg, and I kick him on the inside of his left leg as he stands with all of his weight on it. I hear a snap and know it is broken. I throw several more blows to his midsection, and he falls, rolling on the floor in pain. He is done, but people are throwing beer cans and bottles into the ring, and they don't count him out.

Cameramen are here from the local newspaper ready to take pictures, but when Butch falls, they don't. They really don't want their hand-picked fighter to lose, especially to some dark Italian. Beer cans are thrown in the ring, as an excuse to give their fighter time to recover. His corner helps him up trying to get him ready to continue, but he can't stand and his pain is too great.

His corner steps in and holds up my hand. I look at the cameraman, but he takes no pictures. I want to jump up and shout to celebrate, but I don't want to get the crowd any angrier. Besides, the Sheriff, Redneck and Monroe are shouting enough. They give me my trophy and tie a brown belt with "Champion" on it around me.

I climb out of the ring and stand between the Sheriff and Redneck. With this angry crowd, I, for once, am glad to see them.

Looking at Butch limp toward the locker room, my joy is short lived. He is a warrior, who lets his hate become my hate, making me hurt him much worse than necessary. But it was him or me.

It's time for the main event. Fox steps into the ring, his body chiseled. When Jesse steps in the crowd goes wild, making so much noise I can't hear my own voice. He not only is chiseled, he's also much bigger. There is no way he is eighteen. He has to be at least twenty-five, if he is a day. I wonder how Fox will ever beat this grown man.

They come out of their corners. Jesse is like a raging bull, charging and trying to take Fox out. Fox blocks and dodges his punches, then catches Jesse with a spinning back-kick right on the side of his head, followed by several punches to his solar plexus. Jesse turns and staggers back to his corner.

"How many of them am I fighting? Tell some of 'em to leave," he says. They push him back to the center. Fox snap-kicks him under the chin and he is out cold. It's all over. The crowd is in shock. The cameramen leave without taking any pictures.

But the crowd stands and starts to clap, calling my name. "Reggio! Reggio!" They make me come back into the ring, and all the fighters and the crowd give us a standing ovation. Even Jesse, who is awake now, comes over and jokingly says, "Next time I'm gonna fight y'all one at a time!" Even his corner has to laugh.

The crowd leaves in a hurry. It's been a bad day for White folks in Charleston. Not only have their hand-picked fighters lost the tournament, but even worse they lost their segregated way of life.

The only White folks who are happy are the Sheriff and Redneck, who have won lots of money. Now all we have to do is figure out how to get our five hundred dollars from them, because we're sure they'll come up with some lame excuse.

As we leave the arena, Hawk, one of the old men from behind the café, comes over and shakes our hands. He gives Fox an envelope.

"Cool Papa, don't open this till later. Congratulation on your victory. You sho' made some old men happy," he says.

On our way back to the big house, Fox opens it. A hundred dollar bill falls out with the address of a party, and a note saying 'Please come and help us celebrate our freedom.'

We are so happy and want to shout, but have to be cool till we get our money from the Sheriff.

Later, at the big house, after getting congratulations from

lots of people, we are worn out from the fight and all the excitement. We go upstairs and take a nap. Sometime later there is a knock on the door.

"They're leaving. Y'all come downstairs. Monroe wants to tell you something."

We dress and are downstairs, as the old saying goes, before quick can get ready.

"We're on our way to play golf," Monroe says, "and then go see Johnny Cash tonight. No telling what time we'll get back. Just want to let the champs know the key is under the flower pot in case you go out."

"Mr. Monroe, you are such a nice man. Your Southern hospitality is the best, but ain't you forgettin' something?" Fox asks.

With a frown on his face, scratching his head, "What did I forget?" Monroe asks, just before he begins laughing like crazy.

"Oh you mean the money. You boys have been 'round White people like the Sheriff too long, the kind that keeps their Klan hood in the car trunk. I am very proud to have marched with Martin Luther King and even been spit on by other White people like my old buddy here," he says, patting the Sheriff on the back. "Your money is on the table right beside that nice apple pie my wife made for you."

Bowing with his head down, Fox says, "I am so sorry. Please forgive me."

"Nothing to forgive. You boys take care now and don't give the girls all your money," Monroe says, laughing as he and the Sheriff walk out the door.

On the table is five hundred dollars apiece, more money than we have ever seen in our lives. We are so excited.

We've got all this money, and it's still early.

"Let's go to the party." Fox says.

We hide most of the money, call a cab, and give him the address of the party the man from the café gave us.

19
Street Party

The driver drops us at a blues club called the Blue Light. There are so many people; the crowd has spilled out into the street, so they block off the street and make a street party, celebrating the signing of the Civil Rights Act!

No sooner have we got in the crowd than Hawk, the old man from the café, spots us and tells the crowd we are the champs. They all clap and this older lady brings us a plate of barbecue ribs, greens, potato salad, and two sweet potato pies. We eat so much we can hardly move.

Later, after we recover from all the food, we hear all this laughter from inside the club and go around to the side door. We manage to sneak in far enough to hear this blues man singing. He is a little on the nasty side, but so funny we crack up laughing.

"One leg in the east, one leg in the west, and I'm in the middle doing my best," he sings. "Making love to my woman. She says hurt me baby, so I went upside her head with my guitar."

Then he sings, "My baby said, 'Honey tonight I need nine inches,' so I did it to her three times."

I almost cry when this big man says, "You boys ain't twenty-one. This club is for grown ups. Y'all got to get out of here. Go round back with the young folks."

Reluctantly we leave. As we walk around back James Brown's *Say it loud! I'm Black and I'm proud!* is playing. We quickly forget about the blues singer with so many girls shaking their backsides. These Charleston girls really know how to get funky.

"Tryon is never like this," Fox says.

"Hey them two guys just won the Karate Championship," someone yells.

I feel like a king on a throne with all the clapping and yelling for us. Several pretty girls come over and ask us to dance. Fox goes right out on the floor and is getting down, when it dawns on me I can't dance and feel ashamed as I tell the girls.

"My name is Mary and I like cherries. Let me be your first," she giggles, as she gives me a cup.

"Take a drink of this it will help give you rhythm." I take a spit. It feels like liquid fire going down my insides, but as a karate champ I act like it is nothing.

Mary starts to show me dance steps, and at first I feel like I have two left feet, but the more I drink from the cup the better my dancing gets. Soon I am getting down, at least I think so. Feeling good now, this dancing is so much fun. After all my training, and hard workouts, this dancing is an exercise that is relaxing and fun. Then a slow song comes on called *Oh! What a Night,* by the Dells.

"Let me teach you to slow dance," Mary says. Our bodies become one as she tells me to just follow her.

"This is how you do the belly rub," she says. But it isn't her belly she's using. I am hard as a brick as she grinds on me. She reaches up and kisses me hard. I can taste the alcohol in her kiss as she puts her tongue in my mouth.

"Let's go in the bushes," Mary whispers in my ear. "I am so hot and you are so cute with your hazel eyes, long black hair—and you can fight too."

I am young, but know this means I'm gonna get some. I never thought the Adam test would come so soon, or be so hard. My body says to hell with the Adam test, but how can I go into the bushes with this girl after giving my word to Pops.

I look over at Fox; he is all over this fine Redbone. Walking over to him there's something wrong with the street. I can't seem to walk right.

"Excuse me," I say and pull him away from the girl. "Let's go. Got to get away from here and this dancing is killing me. I'm about to muss up my pants. Let's get the hell out of here."

"Sorry we have to leave. Got to get up early in the morning," Fox tells the girl as we sadly walk toward the cab. The girl is shaking her head and has a funny look on her face, as if she can't believe he can leave her.

"We have to get out of here or somebody's daughter's gonna give up some tonight," I say, stumbling, almost falling on the curb.

"You are high as a Georgia pine." Fox busts out laughing. "That girl got you wasted. At least you got high, these girls giving it away out of both panty legs and we're stuck with this damn Adam test and can't get none. That foxy high yellow girl I was dancing with had a behind softer than drugstore cotton and didn't move my hand when I felt it. Why me Lord, why that damn Adam test? I need to get me some real bad," Fox yells while beating his chest like King Kong.

As we wait on the corner for a taxi, Fox starts to murmur in a low voice. It gets a little louder. He is chanting. "Nam-Myoho-Regne-Kyo, Nam-Myoho-Regne-Kyo."

"Hey! It's bad enough we ain't getting none, but you

done gone Buddhist on me?" I ask.

"No, man! Jade says chanting helps the mind attain a tranquil state. It centers you and gets your mind off worldly things like all this good loving I keep thinking about but can't get."

"Say, man, how does that chant go?" I ask. "Let's chant together, Maybe my hard on will go down."

We get in the taxi and the driver must think we have lost our minds because we chant "Nam-Myoho-Regne-Kyo" all the way back to the big house.

20
Back to Tryon

No sooner do I lie down it seems like the Sheriff is waking us. "Get up! It's time to head back to Tryon," he hollers from downstairs. We get dressed, on our way out. Monroe tells us how much he enjoyed our company.

"Y'all hurry back to see us you hear?" he says, as we drive away. This is the first time I believe a White man really means it.

"Watch me make the Sheriff mad," Fox whispers, as we head through town.

"Hey Sheriff, do this new law mean we can go into any café and eat?"

"Yes, I'm afraid so," he says.

"Can we go in any hotel and sleep in the same bed where White folks sleep?"

"Look, boy, you just about to get on my last nerve. I'm already mad as hell they let you people go to our schools, so you better shut your mouth and quit messing with me. You're gonna find yourself walking back to Tryon," the Sheriff says, sounding like he is about to cry.

"See, I told you I would piss him off," Fox murmurs softly.

Just then he spots the café where just a few days ago a man called him a Nigger.

"Stop. Pull over," he says.

"Give us a few minutes, please, Sheriff." Fox waves at me to come on.

We walk in the front door of the café. All the people stop

talking and eating and look at us like we are gun slingers in an old western movie. We walk over and no sooner do we sit down, the man that called us Niggers a few days ago starts toward us.

"This Cracker's butt is mine," Fox says in a low voice.

Just as the man gets near, he holds out his hand.

"Welcome," he says. "Sorry I called y'all that terrible name, but I've always lived in Charleston, and it's always been a way of life here. Guess you can call it a southern thing. You are raised to think you are better than Black folks and even if you don't believe it, everybody around you lives it! So, it just becomes a part of you. Thank God we are now one America, so we can stop using that awful N word. Please accept my apology by letting me treat you to lunch."

The owner comes over and takes our picture saying we are his first Colored customers.

"I'm gonna put y'all picture in a frame, and put it alongside the picture of the first dollar I made, up yonder on the wall. Besides I hear you kicked that summa bitch Jesse's ass. He struts around here like his ass don't stink. Your lunch is on the house."

I can't believe how nice these White folks are; it's a blessing to know they all aren't like the Sheriff and Redneck. We are having so much fun till the Sheriff sticks his head in the door.

"Let's go! I've got to make another stop. And bring us one of them sweet potato pies and some lemonade to go."

On our way back home after the four best days of my life, I think about so many new things I saw and learned. The ride of my life is in the four-on-the-floor GTO. The big arena. Living in a big house, we see how White people really live.

Even with all that, they don't seem any happier than we do. But, I think the most important thing is all White people even in the south are not racist.

The three-hour ride back home is fine, except the Sheriff has put this redbone hound he won in the back seat with us.

"Sheriff, can't you put this dog in the trunk?" Fox asks. "He's heavy and smells bad. And, can you please play something on the radio except that damn country music?"

"Hell no, Boy! If anybody goes in the trunk, it's one of you! And, I don't play none of that jungle music on my radio, so you best shut your trap 'fore you find yourself walking!"

So the dog lies there with his head on me a while. Then I put his head on Fox. Except for that, we sleep all the way back home.

The Sheriff is on his radio as we pull into town, and we go straight over to the White football field. When we get there, it's a new sight! Something that never happened before in Tryon—White and Colored celebrating together. Even though people are in their own little groups they're still celebrating in the same park. Until today we always did our thing, and they, theirs.

The White high school marching band is playing, but Fox and I are looking at the cheerleaders.

"Do you realize next year them cheerleaders will have some color added to the mix to give them some soul and be even better," Fox says.

"You got that right, and if Jade with her fine self puts on a short cheerleader's outfit, I'll bet you a dollar to a nickel, some old hillbilly is gonna make a country song out of it," I say.

"Yeah, something like the Colored girl with the long black hair wasn't Colored at all," Fox says with a big smile.

"Can you believe we are watching history right before our eyes, going from segregation to integration?" I say. "You want to hear something funny? I can just picture myself sitting down beside an old redneck White man on a bus, watching the expression on his face as I pull a chicken leg out of a brown paper bag and ask him to have some, sir. I am thinking of silly ways to mess with White folks."

As we get out of the car the gang is all over us.

"Y'all kicked some White ass. Showed them Black is beautiful," Sun says. "Wish I could have seen Whitey's face when you went upside his head and showed him Clay ain't the only bad Black brother around."

"I ain't Black, but we did show them Asian and Black is beautiful," Fox says as he pushes Sun aside to hug Jolene.

I head for Jade, thinking there must be a God somewhere to make someone this fine. We have the two finest girls in Tryon, or maybe the whole state of Carolina, all over us.

Fox is kissing Jolene as the Sheriff and Redneck wave our trophies over their heads saying, "We won," as if they had fought someone.

Sheriff pulls us away from the girls telling us we have to go up on the bandstand. Fox grabs the trophy out of his hand putting it in front of him, because he has this hard on from kissing Jolene. I think Adam test or not there is no way he gonna make it much longer before he hits that sexy Jolene. Redneck sees it too and just laughs and laughs.

"Boy, you need to get you some," he says.

We are heroes, both Colored and White shaking our hands, patting us on our backs as we go up on the bandstand.

After our fifteen minutes of fame, the cowbell rings.

"Come and get it!"

They've cooked this pig in a pit under the ground, smothered it in some kicking barbeque sauce and it's so tender it just falls right off the bone. The gang sits around eating BBQ, along with coleslaw and baked beans. We wash it down with sweet tea, and eat peach cobbler on the side.

"Somebody really put their foot in this," I say.

"It's so good, it'll make you smack your mama," Sun says.

"What in the world are you talking about?" Jade asks.

"It's a Colored thing. We have lots of humor in our race," Sun answers. "Food hasta be mighty good to make you smack your mama, 'cause when you do, she gonna kill you."

I pull Fox aside.

"I just want to tell you we have experienced so much in the last few days that many people never get to experience in a lifetime. Pops is right. No amount of money could buy what he has taught us. Without him, we wouldn't be champions and getting all this good treatment. But why did he have to put that cursed Adam test on us?"

What a way to end the best Fourth of July in my life, eating BBQ, sweet potato pie, with friends. Then Jade puts her head full of long black silk-like hair in my lap as we lie on a blanket. Sun has his portable radio on and we listen to Randy's record Mark from Nashville, Tennessee, playing Sam Cook, James Brown, Chuck Berry, and all soul music without a lick of country.

"Nothing could be finer than being in Carolina now that there is no segregation," I tell Fox. "And ending the best four days of my life with my best friends watching fireworks explode in the dark Carolina night."

21
The Sad Goodbye

The next month and a half go by slow and easy, like the summer heat, and I absorb it like a cool glass of lemonade, taking it all in and saying goodbye to all my friends, but especially to some of the characters in Tryon. Two of my favorites have 'shine in their name, but for different reasons.

First, there is Mother Sunshine, a sanctified preacher lady who always carries her tambourine, shouts and hollers 'GLORY' at almost anything. Every time she sees us she hollers, "Glory! You boys been reading your bible?"

If anyone is sick, she shakes her tambourine and prays for them. At the ball game if one of our players gets a hit or makes a basket, she hollers, "Glory" and does her little dance, just like she was shouting in church, while beating her tambourine. Mother Sunshine is a cross between a witch doctor and an Indian medicine man and the best cheerleader Tryon ever had.

But my favorite person is Mrs. Peck who, at a hundred and six, is the oldest person in Tryon. I love to talk to her, ask questions and listen to the stories she tells about slavery. Her mother had been a slave and passed stories down to her. Today I ask her how we started eating chitlins.

She gets a big chuckle out of that. A little brown mule chewing tobacco juice runs out the side of her mouth. She starts talking.

"Child, the old master used to send all the parts of animals he didn't want to the slaves, like backs, necks, gizzards of the chicken, feet, tails, and intestines of the hog, all the parts he called throw away food. The slaves learnt to doctor them up, and put some oxtail or gizzards in a pot of rice, wash and clean the intestines. The old master tasted and then the master started liking the intestines, changed the name to chitlins 'cause he couldn't eat nothin' with a name like hog intestine. Seems he can't stand us to have nothin' of our own, even hog intestine."

My other favorite person with 'shine in their name is an unusual recluse called Shine, who makes the best moonshine in Carolina. He lives way back in the woods and is almost never seen. The Sheriff and everybody in Tryon knows he makes it, but the White folks love his shine so much they never busted him. There are lots of rumors about Shine. One is that he killed a White man in South Carolina after he called him a nasty Nigger. But no one really knows much about him, except he loves to be alone.

I'm his best friend, and when he comes into town about once a month to get supplies for his shine, he always stops by the house. I give him my old comic books and other magazines I pick up from the post office, where people leave them on a table after they finish reading them. And then sometime during the month a basket of apples or some blackberries or fresh fish will appear on the porch, and we know Shine has been there. He doesn't want me to leave, but I assure him Fox will still give Grandma comic books and magazines for him every month.

These are the kind of people I grew up with, the people that make Tryon such a great place. Although I long for the excitement of the big city, I'm having second thoughts about leaving. We will be integrated with the White school and the south is changing. I am thinking about calling Aunt Lucy and telling her I changed my mind. I decide to have a talk with Pops to ask his advice. So the next day we sit down and have lunch in his garden, and I tell him about my misgivings.

After a while, Pops draws his head back and looks off into space.

"Grandson, I am feeling really great. 'Coons used to come over the fence and eat some of my colorful fish. I had to keep chicken wire over the pond to keep them out. Doby got hold of one of them 'coons and I ain't seen hide nor hair of a 'coon since. I've heard you boys talking about that River Heaven, and how beautiful it is down there. I've never been there myself, and would love to go there. I think it's a good day for a hike, and it would help take my mind off these chores I need to be doing around here. What do you say we take a walk down there?"

"Let's go, and bring Larry Doby with you," I say, smiling.

"Good. I will get us some water," Pops says.

"No, don't. We don't need any. There is a spring the Indians made with the coolest, sweetest water you ever drank, flowing right out of the earth."

In the woods I am surprised to see how much Pops knows about nature. Little things like where a chipmunk burrows in his hole or spotting a hornet nest way up in a tree. It is a joy walking and listening to him and watching Doby run with the excitement of a young colt let out in the pasture for the first time.

"Son, look at that big redheaded woodpecker over there

pecking on that tree. Did you know there was a person who didn't believe in God changed their mind after watching a woodpecker?"

"Come on now, Pops! How could that happen? I know you have some great stories, and they all have a message, but this time I think it's a little far out."

"They reasoned that after the first woodpecker pecked a tree, he would get a headache and get worms off the ground, or eat berries like other birds," Pops says. "But, woodpeckers have especially designed heads with shock absorbers so they don't get headaches and their beaks are especially designed too. So there must be a designer. That's how they started believing in God. It's a true story," .

Pops' stories are so good it seems like we arrive at Heaven in a much shorter time than usual. We found a picture-perfect seat on the bank of the river.

"Just look in the water and clear your mind, and just let it talk to you," Pops says.

I do, and the sound of the rushing water reminds me of rain on a tin roof. After a while, I'm feeling pretty peaceful.

Pops is quiet for a long time, just looking at the river. Finally, he speaks.

"You know, you can't cross the same river twice." He looks at me sideways, pausing for a moment. "By the time you start back across, it has changed, and War, *you* have changed. Ever think about that? Even Doby has changed. See how he looks across the field where you said he came from? He has a chance to return to his old ways, but you see how close he stays to me. Even he knows change can be good."

I shake my head from side to side.

"No, never thought about it, but you're right. It's never the same water and after Charleston, and winning the championship, neither am I."

22

Trynots

"Do you know how Tryon got its Name?" Pops asks. I tell him, "Yes they were building a road down the mountain, and kept running into rock, making it hard to cut. They would say we have to keep trying on. We just have to Tryon."

"That's the White man story. I'm about to tell you the real one....You see those Trynots stuck to the bank? Don't want to try anything new. Too scared to let go."

I don't see anything, but I play along with Pops to hear his story.

"One day a young one got tired of putting so much effort into not trying. Of course, he was into martial arts and he said to himself, 'This is no way to live, stuck here on this bank. I'm going to let go.' You see, he wanted more out of life than just being a Trynot. He was going to let go. Anything would beat staying here stuck to this bank, day after day, he figured.

"The other Trynots resisted, of course. 'But our food flows right to us here,' they sniveled. 'We've got it made! Besides, if you let go you'll smash on the rocks and be killed.'

"But he wanted more than just being stuck to a bank, and just couldn't get the courage to do it. Then one day a martial arts book flowed by, and after reading it, he became a brave warrior like you and let go. After some bumps and bruises, he came up in this calm lake. Looking around, at the trees, the flowers and all the wonders of the earth. He couldn't wait to head back upstream to tell all the Trynots to let go.

"When he got there, he looked over the edge of the bank, into the river. The Trynots looked up at him and said, 'He looks like us, but he must be a God,' and refused to let go. How hard he tried to tell them about all the wonders waiting for them if they only let go.

"Grandson, I had to let go of my old country when I came here. My son and his wife were killed. That's how I got Fox and Jade. But that's another story I will tell you when we have lots of time.

"Right now, Grandson, don't be a Trynot! Let go and Tryon. Follow your destiny. There are a lot of new and exciting things waiting for you in the city. Tryon and I have taught you well, and we would like for you to stay, but the River Heaven has spoken. It's city time for you, my grandson."

I just sit there a few minutes, letting his message sink in. I so want to ask him about how his son got killed and how he got Fox and Jade, but knew this was not the time. We are silent for several minutes.

I see tears in Pops' eyes, as if remembering his son's death still pains him after all these years.

Pops breaks the silence.

"In my old country, we parents sometimes chose who our children would marry. We would have chosen you for Jade, but she has chosen you for herself. Her love for you is so strong, she will be here when you return. And so will I. Go to the city and become a young man. See and learn new and exciting things, and come back and tell me about your adventures."

After that talk, I'm ready to go. As we walk back to Pops' house, I have feelings of loving him the same as for a real father.

It's my last night in Tryon, and Fox and I go up on a high hill I call my spot and talk about how we will always be best friends, and if one of us makes it in life we will always look out for the other.

Fox pulls out a bottle of Pops' sake and sets it on the ground. He takes a small knife and cuts his arm, and then he gives me the knife and I do the same. We put our cuts together like the Apache Indian warriors Cochise in the movie *Broken Arrow*, and become blood brothers.

Then we drink sake and lie back and watch the stars, so big and close in the Carolina night, it seems like you could reach up and touch them. We give our thanks to the Creator for our friendship and spend the rest of the night talking about all the fun we had being buddies, and saying our goodbyes.

23
Going Up North

It's early, well before dawn, when the big Buick sedan pulls out. Leaving Tryon is one of the most exciting, yet saddest days of my life.

My Aunt Lucy and her husband, Uncle Jim, are taking me to the big city to live with them. She will be my new mother.

Her sister, my real mother, was only nineteen when she died shortly after my birth. Her mother, the only one I have ever known, has raised me from a baby until now.

My real mother was very light complexioned, and very pretty, but still considered Colored. When I was born, Grandma told me, my mother got real sick and the hospital didn't treat her. Instead, they gave her some aspirin, told her to go home and rest. Mother got worse. Grandma called the doctor, who didn't show up for days.

Shortly thereafter, my mother asked to hold me one more time, kissed me on the forehead, handed me to Lonnie, my father, and died. He was twenty-one and they had only been married a little over a year. Grandma told me this was one of the saddest funerals 'Black or White' Tryon ever had. So many young people were at the funeral and in this small town she was like a best sister to them.

At the funeral, Grandma told me my father tried to take my mother out of the casket. She said it was not a pretty sight. Lonnie knocked over flowers, pushed away people trying to console him and had to be forced away from the casket. He stormed out of the church went home, got his gun and was on his way to the hospital to kill the doctor and half the hospital staff for not treating her, and letting her die like an animal. His brother and several other people had to jump him, tie him up, and put him in the back seat of our cousin's car. The cousin took him back up north to live with him. Lonnie for sure would've killed lots of White folks and been lynched in the process.

Every Christmas Lonnie sends me presents, and often sends Grandma money.

I was about four when he came to visit me, but he didn't stay long. I cried when he left. I had Grandma, but no real mother, and it seemed as if my father didn't like me. Later in life we sat down for a long talk and he told me it was too hard for him to see me. I reminded him too much of my mother. Thank goodness, now when he sees me, he can't stop smiling. He's always talking about how proud he is of me.

After a long hug, a few prayers, a bag of fried chicken, and Grandma telling me for the hundredth time to be a good boy, we are on our way to the big city for a new and hopefully exciting life.

The ride north is a lesson in geography as I watch the terrain change from lots of trees and rolling hills to flat land and back again. Houses and people are much closer together than in the south. We could stop and eat at any restaurant now. To have White waitresses wait on us and call Uncle Jim "Sir" is a nice treatment I am not accustomed to. I smile to myself at the way the waitress talks without a southern accent.

24

Home In The Big City

My excitement mounts as we pull into the city. The tall buildings already have their night-lights on. Their silhouettes remind me of lightning bugs blinking in the trees at dusk in the Blue Ridge Mountains.

Shortly we come to this really nice neighborhood with big houses. I know this has to be a White neighborhood, but unlike in the south, I hope a few Black families live here. I wonder if one of the houses is my aunt's. Soon we arrive at this huge apartment building and pull up to the front door.

"This is your new home. Let's unload the car," Uncle Jim says.

Getting out of the car, a funny smell permeates the air, as if something is burning. It stings my eyes. I ask Auntie what's burning.

"The air pollution is high today," she laughs.

As I look around, there is concrete everywhere, almost like the earth is made of it instead of dirt. I wonder what the apartment looks like.

We enter the hallway. Uncle Jim takes out a key and opens a door on the right.

"We take care of this place," he says, as we step down into this hallway. He points to a room off to the left.

"Put your things in there. That's your room."

It is small, but nice and quiet. He and Aunt Lucy go down the hall to where their room is. I feel happy because I will be alone. Besides that, there is a big dresser drawer with a large mirror, a nice sized closet and a big bed with a new mattress. Lucy has gone out of her way to make me comfortable.

We unload, and then I take a quick bath. Trying to lather up, I think something is wrong with the soap, because there is no lather. This is very different from Tryon where the water is soft and makes lots of lather. I like to lie in the warm water and use Ivory soap because it make a lot of suds and floats on top of the water. However, I see a black ring around the tub and no suds.

After getting dressed, I make my way to where Aunt Lucy is in the kitchen busy preparing a meal.

"What's wrong with the water?" I ask her.

"Nephew, because of all of the chemicals they put in to purify it, the water is hard. Don't worry! It's safe to drink and you'll get used to it."

"Now I know why it also smells and when you take a drink it has a funny taste," I say.

With hard water, pollution, and concrete everywhere it seems like the city is built by men. And Tryon, which is so natural with soft clean water, tall trees, flowers and birds everywhere, is made by God. So, my first night in the city except for my nice room is not so good.

The next day everything changes. The hometown baseball team is in town. Aunt Lucy buys me a bus pass and shows me how to catch the bus; I transfer from one bus to another in order to get to the baseball stadium, and I go see my first Major League baseball game. It is so thrilling to see real Major League baseball, eat a real ballpark hot dog, but I still miss Mother Shine doing her little dance and hollering "Glory!"

After the game, I walk down to the Boys' Club, where they have an indoor basketball court, showers, pool tables, and all kinds of play things. But the best part is, it doesn't matter if you are White or Colored.

This is the way life is supposed to be, without all that Jim Crow stuff in the South. It even gets better. On my way back home, there is a grade school with an outside basketball court on this big playground. Lots of boys, both Colored and White, are playing. Now the city is all I hoped for.

I walk down to the court and the tallest boy who is Black, stops the game and walks over to me.

"Are you a light skinned punk who sucker-punched his friend last week at the party?"

Another boy walks up, saying, "Yeah, that's the punk! Let's kick his butt!"

"Fellows, I just got here from Carolina. I've never been to a party. I just want to play a little basketball, but if you want to fight, let me warm up a little."

I go through my karate, stopping momentarily to watch their faces as I kick and punch the air so fast it makes Cassius Clay look slow.

When I finish, the tall Black kid looks at the other kid.

"I don't think this is the one who sucker-punched our buddy."

"You're right," the other kid says. "Besides, he's from Carolina."

The tall kid holds out his hand.

"My name is Reggie. Welcome to the neighborhood. Introduce yourself to the rest of the fellows and you can play on my team."

"Thanks," I say, and after a few "Hellos," the boys are

really nice.

"I just want to watch today," I say and go to sit on a bench.

25
Markey the Jew

As I watch the boys play basketball, I notice off to the left sitting in the grass, is a well dressed young boy. He has a little round cap on his head, reading a book. A black and white dog lies beside him. I just have to go over and ask about the little cap. I walk up.

"What's with your hat?" I ask.

"I am Jewish," he says, and keeps reading his book without looking up.

"Excuse me, but you are the first Jew I ever met. To me, except for the little hat, you seem like any other White person."

He looks up.

"Being a Jew isn't about color. It's a way of life, a religion."

We talk for a while and he is very friendly, but laughs almost every time I speak. I am beginning to wonder if he is a little bit off.

"Why do you keep laughing almost every time I say something?"

"I'm laughing at your southern accent, and some of the words you say like down yonder, or little bitty."

We both laugh because until then, I don't realize I have an accent.

"My name is Markey, but you can just call me Mark."

"Mark, you still haven't told me why you wear that funny little hat?"

"Without going into a long explanation, the short of it is to show respect to our God, to give respect and acknowledge there is someone higher than I. I haven't seen you around. Are you new to the neighborhood?"

"I sure am. Maybe you can show me around sometime. I live down the street in the big apartment building."

"I would love to. I'll be up here about ten tomorrow. If you show up, we can do something. But I must go now and do some chores. Come, Teton," he says. His dog gets up and walks right beside him.

The rest of the week goes fast. I meet and play with the boys on the basketball court. We all have a good laugh when one of the boys accidentally fouls me going for the basketball, and jokingly says, "I'm sorry. Please don't use none of that kung fu stuff on me."

After a great workout playing basketball, I sleep like a baby that night.

The next day Mark takes me to a big swimming pool, with a high diving board and lots of Black and White girls in bathing suits. Sitting down on the edge of the pool, looking at all the pretty girls, I think swimming in the River Heaven is great fun, but with all these foxy girls walking around in tight swimming suits, this is like recess in Heaven. Just as I begin to learn my way around the city and have so much fun, my fun is cut short when school starts.

26
New School

I walk up to what looks to me like a college instead of a high school. There are almost two thousand students, about the number of all the people in Tryon. To make matters worse, most of them are White.

As the weeks pass, I quickly learn two things: First, these White people are different than the ones in the South where we call White folks rednecks, Crackers, and poor White trash. Here they are from many parts of the world with many different cultures, such as Jewish, Polish, Irish, English, Italian and Asian. Most have their own part of town, which enhances the city culture, and have restaurants that serve food from the country. However, they are all still White except a few Asians. I have never seen anything like it.

The coloreds here are called Blacks. The names Negro and Colored seem to be names of the past. Between classes, Blacks meet at a place they affectionately call among themselves "Coon's Corner". It's not a nice name, maybe someone's idea of a joke, but at least I can go there between classes, meet and associate with some Black folks.

The second thing I learn from my different schooling in Tryon is the system back there is set up for Colored folks to fail. I am so far behind in my classes that the lessons are like Greek to me.

27
Black History

The Colored school in Tryon taught us about Booker T. Washington, an ex-slave and how in 1881 he founded Tuskegee Institute in the Black belt of Alabama. Tuskegee is a Black college that launched the careers of thousands of Blacks. He may have been the most powerful Black man in U. S. history.

George Washington Carver was also born a slave. In 1896, he became the head of Tuskegee's Agriculture Department and revolutionized farming in the south with his crop combinations and new use for peanuts and sweet potatoes.

Frederick Douglas, also born a slave, used to run races against the cat and dog to reach the bones that were tossed out of the slave owner window. He later became the Martin Luther King of his day.

I knew a little North Carolina history, with some lightweight math and a little English. This is great if you are Black, or plan to live the rest of your life in North Carolina. But none of that stuff is any good up north. In English they talk about conjugating a sentence and in math, solving compound fractions, something I never heard of. If that isn't bad enough, the history really gets me. I'm supposed to know when this White man crossed the Delaware River some time back in eighteen something, or when was the battle of the Spanish American War. I don't even know there was one.

Two things save me. One is Markey. We walk to school together even though it is over a mile. By the time we walk to catch one bus, and then transfer to another, it is easier to just walk to school. On the way, Mark explains the lessons to me, and teaches me other things about city life, like which neighborhoods to stay out of.

The second is my Uncle Jim who helps me with my homework. He teaches me math, because I have no idea how to work even simple common fractions. He teaches me to understand nouns and pronouns in English. Uncle is a lifesaver, one of the most educated, yet dumbest men I have ever met in my life.

In his little room down the hall, pictures of awards he received in high school are hanging on the wall. Uncle Jim was number two in his high school graduating class, a chess club member, a debate club member, and a real brain.

Even more unbelievable, he graduated in the top ten percent of his class from the university. Uncle seems to love teaching me, as if he has flashbacks reminding him just how smart he really is. This is a blessing for me.

However, looking at him today, always dressed in old wrinkled denims with a lit cigarette in his mouth and butts all over his funky nasty little room, it seems such a waste.

My aunt really likes her job. She works for a doctor and his family, cooking, cleaning and driving their kids to school. She has the weekends off. She always makes me go to church on Sundays, but Uncle Jim never goes.

One day he comes in half drunk, talking to himself. He staggers down to his room. This seems like a good time to get him to talk about his degree. I just have to know how such a smart man can sink so low. So I enter his nasty little room.

"Hey, Uncle! How are you doing?"

"I'm fine, but it's already cold as a well-digger's asshole outside. I had to get me a little antifreeze, if you know what I mean."

With him in a talkative mood, I point to his degree on the wall.

"Uncle, what subject did you get your degree in?"

"Nephew, lots of good that damn degree did me. Everywhere I go the companies are impressed with me, and they all want to hire me. But to be head of the janitor department, or some low paying job over Negroes, but never over any White people. Despite all my degrees I am still a Black man. Things are opening up a little bit now after integration, but I'm too damn old to meet the man every day. So if the only job I could get is in the janitor department, hell, I might as well be a caretaker of this big apartment, where I can at least be my own boss. I did not spend all those days and nights studying when I could have been out chasing ladies to have some dumb-assed White man with a high school diploma say 'Boy, go down yonder and sweep my corner office.' You see, nephew, I just couldn't stand that, so, here I am!"

"Uncle, you know what? I've been told how great it is up north for Blacks, and in many ways it is. But it seems like what they did to you is the cruelest form of segregation. Even more than in the South, because there you know the White man has his foot up your butt. But here, he lets you climb all the way to the top before he pulls the ladder from under you."

After that talk, I understand the hurt Uncle feels from being treated so bad just because he's Black. I gain total respect for Uncle. I wonder how much the world has lost by keeping so many brilliant Black men down.

The next few months go by slowly. It seems like the schoolwork gets harder each day. The weather is getting colder and colder.

The only thing that saves me from going mad is I make the freshmen basketball team and after class can take out my loneliness on the court. But the long walk home alone in the cold dark and the unbelievable amount of homework take most of the fun out of that. Nevertheless, it seems the bad outweighs the good.

28
Homesick

I couldn't believe my ears hearing Nat King Cole singing the Christmas Song this early in the season. Being so homesick, my mind is made up to catch the first thing smoking back to Tryon as soon as school lets out for the Christmas holidays. Just sitting here, feeling depressed, looking out at the snow steadily falling, I'm trying to figure out how to tell Lucy I'm going back home for Christmas.

My favorite singer, Sam Cook, is singing *Darling, You Send Me* on the radio when the DJ stops the song and says he has some bad news. Sam Cook has been shot and killed by some jealous lady in a hotel room.

I have been doing homework, but I'm starting to go stir-crazy sitting in the house. Along with this bad news about Sam, even though it's freezing outside, I just must get out. I put on my boots, get my heavy coat and my Russian style hat with the fur that covers my ears and catch a bus going to some part of the city I have never seen before.

I look out the window at snow falling like white rain-drops. Some people already have Christmas decorations up, and with the lightly falling snow, they make a joyful and glorious sight from inside the warm bus.

Already feeling better, I almost miss the sign saying martial arts lessons. At the next stop, I get off and run back to the building. Opening the door, I step into the most beautiful Dojo I have ever seen. There are big mirrors on the walls where you can watch your workouts, punching bags, mats on the floor. This is some Dojo.

A group of kids are throwing punches. Taking off my coat and boots for a moment makes me feel like going over to challenge the whole school.

But instead, I walk over, and show one of the young boys the correct way to throw a punch. I feel this strong tug on my arm as the instructor asks me in a very loud voice, "What the hell are you doing?" He has a look in his eye like he wants to punch me; for a minute I think about challenging him.

Instead I back off, walk over to a mat and start to do my Kata. This is a wonderful new experience watching myself throw punches in front of a wall of mirrors, revealing glimpses of just how beautiful I look doing my techniques. As I punch and kick, it feels good, like I am back in Tryon with Pops and Fox. It is at this moment I realize just how homesick I really am, and I put on a hell of a show. I even go over and break a few boards.

When I finish my Kata I hear this big applause.

"Who is your teacher?" The instructor asks, "You are one of the best young fighters I have ever seen."

I tell him of my training in Tryon with Pops, and Pops' history in martial arts.

"Great. Do you want to help me teach part of the class on Saturdays? You could help so much and I will pay you well," he says.

I jump at the chance. This will not only give me money, but also help take my mind off the hard schoolwork. It will also help get me through this even harder cold winter. Most of all, it gives me a chance to practice martial arts in a state-of-the-art Dojo.

Riding home, I feel warm and happy, even though it is freezing outside. As I look out the window, I see that some people already have their Christmas lights on. I am beginning to get the Christmas spirit and the thought of going home to Tryon fades away.

29
1965

Out with the old and in with the new, is my attitude. As Mark and I walk to school each day I think about how different we are. I'm into sports; Mark is into academics. Still, we have become best friends.

Old Man Winter slowly lets go and spring comes. There are no dogwood trees or colorful flowers everywhere like in Tryon. One day it just gets warm.

John, a tall skinny Black kid, and I make the basketball team. We are the only freshmen to practice with the varsity team and if they get a nice lead we even play.

After basketball, in the spring we want to run track and play baseball together. Unfortunately, you can't play both. So John chooses track and I, baseball. We have become good friends and he is my new running buddy.

Finally, school is out. I get my report card, and I pass. Much to my surprise, I have become a very good student. Now I look forward to going to Tryon. The very next week sitting at the dinner table I am the happiest I have been since moving to the city. I play enough quarters, usually at the end of a game or when the team gets a big lead, to get a letter in basketball. Lucy sewed it on this nice white sweater and I can't wait to go to Tryon and show it off.

Next week after church we are sitting around the dinner table when Aunty says, "War, I have some bad news about going home. With you here, plus we had to buy a new car, our funds are a little low. We are sorry but we can't go home until next year."

I don't want to believe what she says. Another year without seeing Grandma, Jade, and all the gang turns my joy into sadness.

However the sadness doesn't last long. I get to see girls in their tight suits at the swimming pool and I hang out with John and sometimes Markey. Plus, I play American Legion baseball, and with all the things to do at the boys club, the city has captured me. Now it's my new home.

The next year is more of the same, only better. John and I are starting on the basketball team. I play centerfield in baseball and even quarterback a little, in football.

In June 1966, school is out and I am sixteen. Over six feet tall and more than 200 pounds of pure muscle. I can't wait to go to Tryon and show myself off.

Fox is eighteen now and getting married on July 3rd. I am to be his best man. Afterwards, everybody who ever attended the Colored school is invited to one last big reunion before they close it. Fox's reception is part of the big celebration.

There is even talk that Nina Simone, the great singer from Tryon, might come.

Fox and I are scheduled to put on a martial arts demonstration. I have talked about Tryon so much with Markey that he wants to know if he can visit with me. Because of work, Lucy can't go to Tryon until later in the year. So, I am going to ride the bus to Tryon...until Mark knocks on my door.

"War, my parents are going to Florida for a long overdue vacation. They can drop us off, then pick me up in two weeks after their vacation. I've never been south and would love to walk in the woods and swim in the River Heaven you always talk about. Do you think I can go with you?"

"Sure! This will work out great because Auntie is coming down later to visit and take me back to the city. Let me call Grandma and ask if it is okay." I make the phone call and she says, yes. So in a few more days, we will go to Tryon. I can't wait.

30
The Goddess

One of my chores in the apartment is to pick up the rubbish every Tuesday and Friday. I take a burlap sack and go up the fire escape in the back of the building. Each apartment has a landing there, where people keep a small garbage can.

I spread the burlap, empty the cans, and then carry it to the next landing. By the time I get it to the top it's full. I tie the ends together then hold it out over the railing as long as I can in my right hand. I watch as my muscles swell and bulge. Then I switch to my left hand as long as I am able to, and then drop it down to the alley. I later transfer it to the bins in the alley for the trash collectors to pick up.

At the top, sits one larger apartment, which is more like a penthouse. I remember at fourteen, the second time I picked up rubbish there, this young White lady opens the door and steps out on the landing. The early morning sunlight reflects through her hair to make her body glow like a goddess.

As she hands me a bag of rubbish, I steady myself because I have never been this close to such a beautiful White lady. She has on a very short white robe showing her long shapely legs.

Then, only a few days earlier, I had lived in the South, and still had images in my mind of a photograph in *Jet* magazine of Emmett Till, a fourteen-year-old boy, the same age as me at the time, from Chicago, lying in an open-coffin. He had been beaten beyond recognition by White men in Mississippi for just whistling at a White woman. In the South, you might get hung being this close, but she is very nice and now two years later we are good friends

This is my last rubbish pick up before leaving for Tryon. When I get to the top of the landing and her apartment, she opens the door with a bag in her hand.

"Good morning, young man. You really have filled out since that little skinny kid I met a few years ago," she says. "I made you some cookies to take on your trip. Your uncle told me you were leaving tomorrow. Don't forget to send me a postcard, if you can leave those southern girls alone long enough."

I try to speak, but the words won't come out. As I reach for the cookies, her robe is slightly open and I can see her red bra and white panties as she hands the cookies to me. I manage to say thank you in a low voice, and want to say more but words won't come out.

She smiles, waits a few seconds to see if I say something, and says, "Have a safe trip. See you when you get back," and goes back in the house. I know she showed me her titties on purpose, and maybe if I wasn't too slow to take the hint, I could be playing with them now.

I go to bed early to rest for the trip tomorrow, and dream about the white panties and titties in the red bra all night.

It is early the next morning when Markey calls and says he isn't sure he is going. My heart skips a beat. I ask, "What's wrong?"

"There is no way I can stand to leave my dog in a kennel for two weeks," he says.

"Mark, bring your dog. Tryon has lots of woods and

space for him to run. We can take him through the woods to Heaven. Let him chase a little squirrel or something. Let him be a real dog for a change. Teton will love it."

"I sure am glad you said that. I am so excited. We will pick you up in about fifteen minutes, as soon as I get Teton's stuff together," Mark says.

As we hit the highway for the ten hour trip, I drift off into a peaceful sleep, dreaming about how everyone will look after two years. When I wake, I notice the ride south is a thing of beauty. I watch the changes of the different houses and landscape. I can't wait to arrive in Tryon.

31
The Cemetery Side

Mark's father is such a fast driver, there is still daylight left as we enter Tryon. We hit the Colored section of town, which is called the Cemetery Side because when you enter the town the Baptist and the Methodist churches are almost side-by-side, and across the street is the county cemetery.

The funny thing is that all the White people are buried in the front of the cemetery with mausoleums, statues and well-manicured lawns.

The Colored people are buried down on the hillside in the back, on the other side of the road that runs through the cemetery, as if this road makes a difference to the dead White people.

Shortly, we pass the storefront, the old gathering place where everybody hangs out. They holler my name as we pass. When we pull up to the house, Grandma comes out, hugs me and starts talking about how I have grown.

"Welcome," she says, "come on in. Rest a while. Supper is on the stove."

Markey's dad says, "We can't stay long, but since you already cooked, if it's not too much trouble, we could stand a bite to eat."

"No trouble at all. I hope you like Southern food. I cooked a mess of greens, fried chicken, and some candied sweet potatoes. I even picked the blackberries myself for your cobbler."

Mark's parents are very impressed with the down-home meal. They stay some, but are soon on their way to Florida. I can't wait to head for Fox's house, but I know we must talk to Grandma for a while. Soon she senses we are getting restless and says, "Y'all get now. I know you want to go see your buddies. But don't you boys be stayin' out late."

We take off. Markey's dog, Teton, is a border collie and he is running all through the bushes having a great time until we come to the gate of Fox's house. Doby is barking and raising hell. Then he recognizes me, even after two years, and starts wagging his tail. As I open the gate and enter, he is all over me; licking and making me pet him.

Pops, Fox, and Jade come out at the same time, all trying to hug me. I hug Jade first as we hop around while everybody is trying to talk at once, with Doby barking. We are quite a sight. Although I am an only child, I know this is my true family.

We have forgotten about Markey when Jade asks, "Who is your friend? Tell him to come in."

Neither he nor Teton would budge until they put Doby up. We all talk for a while, then Fox wants to take the run. I know that means he wants to be alone to talk with me.

Markey says he will be fine and stays to talk to Pops and Jade. So, we start to run, but soon slow to a walk. I tell him about me starting on all the teams and how I am a star. It is great fun talking and catching up on the last two years.

"Jolene still hasn't given me any. I don't know how I put up with that 'wait till we get married' bullshit this long. But we will be married in two days and those long pretty legs will be mine. I'm going to get some by the lake, up in the mountains, and everywhere in between to make up for lost

113

time," Fox says with a smile.

It is dark when we get back; so, we all say goodnight. Markey and I go home and straight to bed.

32
Second Day Home

Getting up to a real home-cooked breakfast is a small taste of Heaven. It only gets better as I see my cousins drive up. They live down in the country in a little town called Pea Ridge. We hug and kiss; then we sit down on the porch laughing and telling stories for a while.

"So many people ask me to bring you by their house," my cousin Jimmie says. "Let's take a ride."

It's great fun having him drive Grandma and me around visiting friends and relatives. I could eat, slip out back for a little drink and not have to worry about me or Grandma driving us back home after dark with her bad eyes.

Mark says Jade has asked him to help her do something, so he doesn't go with us. It is almost dark when we get back. As we pass the gathering place, I hear Sun holler, "Hey, War! Get out!" So we stop.

I get out and Jimmie takes Grandma on home. As I walk up, I am greeted like a long lost brother. As everybody hugs and shakes my hand, it is almost as if I never left. Several big boys are crying.

"Hey, fellows. I know you're glad to see me, but why you tearing up?" I say.

"We just got the word. Candy was killed in Vietnam," one of the boys says.

"Just think about all that sweet pipe gone to waste," Sun says. "I know women are crying all over Carolina. My boy Candy died for what? He should have kept his butt here.

Over there fighting for Whitey. He sure didn't die for us."

"I heard about it before I left home, and brought some of Pops' sake. So, everyone, let's drink to Candy," Fox says.

We all pour some on the ground and drink to the Candy Man.

After things quiet down, Fox, Head, Sun and I walk a piece until we are alone.

"I have a bone to pick with you," Sun says. "Even though you've been gone for two years, you're still my best buddy, and I would take a bullet for you. But why you bring some White boy down here into our section of town? If any of the brothers bring anything White down here it's a woman. But you bring a dude! You have a thing with that boy? You must be hitting that round eye. You done turned queer on us? You went up north and come back home with a little sugar in you tank."

They all laugh at Sun giving me a hard time. Then Sun says, "If that wasn't bad enough the White boy has been seen with Jade. He might hit that thing before you. But don't worry, because as soon as I see him, I am going to wipe his White ass and send him back up North on the first thing smokin'."

I don't see Mark as White, I guess because being mixed myself, people are people. But, this is the South. I quickly change the subject because I know how Sun hates White people.

Soon we have a great time talking about old times and how we are going to drink and act like fools at Fox's reception.

It feels so good being back home. As I walk up to the house, Mark comes running down the path to meet me, laughing.

"Smell my finger," he says, as he puts it up to my nose. "I put my finger in it and I could've got some, but didn't have a rubber. Where can I get a rubber?"

I step back to keep from smelling his funky finger and to keep from breaking his jaw, at that moment. I feel Sun is right. White folks are dogs.

"Rebecca is so sexy with her big legs and that nice big round butt," Mark says. "She's gonna give me some. You got any rubbers?"

I don't think he knows how close he comes to getting knocked out because I thought he is talking about Jade. I haven't spent much time with her. Maybe she is mad at me, wants to get back at me. Then I realize Sun and all of his hatred of the White man talk has me thinking crazy.

Mark is my friend, and Jade has more class than that. He is talking about Rebecca, the Black girl I had my first and only sex with, although I didn't finish it.

I feel a great relief.

"Come on Mark," I say. "Let's go over to the storefront and get some rubbers, or condoms as you White boys call them."

I feel relieved because Mark is going to get some from Rebecca, and Jade is still my girl. I will make sure I spend some time with her tomorrow.

33
Sun Versus Mark

As we walk to the storefront, all the fellows are still there. Sun comes rushing up to Mark and says, "This is the Colored section of town. We don't allow White boys over here."

I step in and say, "He is my guest. Now you can talk about him, his momma, his dog or his thing, but no one had better lay a hand on him. Y'all are my boys and I love you, but if you touch Mark, I will be on you like white on rice. If you want to fight with him, do it in words. Keep your hands off him."

"White people in 1865 claimed to set us free," Sun lit into Mark, "but it isn't until almost a hundred years later in '54 before we had the right to go to school with y'all and the South has been slow doing even that.

"It wasn't until '64 before they made it a Civil Rights Act, and it's still not a law, but the Act gives us rights we should have had a hundred years ago. Now we can eat, go to the same bathroom as you suckers. In '65, you all had our leader Malcolm X killed. I know the true story—the White man was behind it."

Then I see in Mark a side I have never seen before. I guess because of my presence, he isn't afraid. He lit into Sun like a pit bull.

"It's your own Black people who killed Malcolm," he says, "and your people are not the only people who had it hard. If you think White people are only hard on Blacks you must not know how they hate Jews. Have you ever heard of Auschwitz?"

"Hell, no. What is that, some kind of sickness? And anyhow what's that got to do with anything?" Sun asked.

"Auschwitz was a death camp where over a million Jews were put in gas chambers or crematorium and killed. I'm sure you heard of the Holocaust?" says Mark. "In case you haven't heard, over six million Jews were killed by Whites, and other Whites let it happen. Jews were loaded into box cars like cattle and shipped off to death camps like Auschwitz. All the Air Force had to do was bomb the railroad tracks to stop it, but so-called White America never did a damn thing. They bomb everything in Germany except the train tracks leading to the death camps." Mark takes a breath.

"Since you are talking about my people, tell me this about yours," Mark pauses. "Up North, I know this real big beautiful church your people go to. Every Sunday they put big money in the collection plate, yet all around this big church, the houses and people are in bad shape. Maybe you can tell me what your people get out of putting all that money in the church when they're so poor, and no one seems to benefit but the preacher? Have you ever seen a preacher driving a Volkswagen?"

"I'm all ears. Can't wait to hear Sun answer this one. Looks like your friend Mark won round one," Fox says.

"The church has kept the Black people together all through slavery," Sun says. "Even today it's the only place we can get away from you White devils and be ourselves. Here we can sing our own gospel and spiritual songs, jump up and down, shout, and praise the Lord with soul. Not sit quietly in a pew, stiff as a board, like you no soul, White folks do."

Head steps in, "Sun, shut up. Enough is enough. Lighten up fellows. Our buddy War is back in town. Let's hear what he's been doing the last couple of years. And his friend is a Jew. He ain't no real White boy anyway."

We talk a little longer among ourselves. Sun and Mark are still into that Black and White thing and go off to the side. It seems like they are becoming friends. We start telling dirty jokes, and talk about girls for a long time, before heading for home.

As I get close to home I keep thinking it seems in Tryon the boys are always talking about getting some, but up north it's kind of on the back burner.

I look over at Mark. He has dropped back and is walking around in circles looking up in the night sky.

"I can't believe it. I can't believe all those things up in the sky. I've never seen anything like all those stars. The Big Dipper is so clear. I never knew there were so many bright stars. It's such a mind blowing, awesome sight. So many people in the city never see this great sky show. I'm so glad I came to Tryon. You are so lucky to be born here," he says.

"You know what, Mark? You're right, Tryon is a gem."

34
Mrs. Peck

It's about nine in the morning when I hear this knock on the door; Grandma has gone to town and let us sleep. I get up to open the door. It's Shine.

"Mrs. Peck sent word for you to come see her," he says. We talk a while.

"I can't stay long. Got to go to town and get my supplies," he says.

As he leaves I hug him. Shine smells like sour beer and very funky. I love this smelly moonshine-making man, even if he doesn't take baths very often. We say our goodbyes, perhaps for the last time, and I watch as he disappears down the road.

I head for Mrs. Peck's.

When I arrive, she's sitting in her rocking chair, rocking back and forth, with a cup of hot toddy sitting on the table beside her.

Her body is very frail, her face wrinkled and weather-beaten from the sun and old age. But her eyes hold a glow of peace. I sit down on the ground in front of her.

"How are you doing, Mrs. Peck?"

She rocks more, then says in an old timey, Black southern drawl, "I'm just like this rockin' chair, movin' back and forth, but ain't goin' nowhere. I heard you was in town, so I sent word for you to come see me. Son, you've been real good to me, bringin' me funny books." She always calls comics funny books.

"You were always goin' gettin' my Brown Mule chewing tobacco, and all, even when I wasn't supposed to have it. Them doctors took me off Brown Mule years ago, but they all been dead so long what did they know? I know I figures pretty good, but never could hardly read or write, but love to look at pictures in them funny books. So I want to give you a present."

She hands me a solid gold pocket watch with a long silver chain and says, "This is yours for being so good to me."

"I can't take this," I stutter.

Mrs. Peck spit out some tobacco juice, took a sip of her hot toddy.

"Boy, hush up! Don't you sass me. My mama was a slave and took this watch from her old master right after he raped her, but in those days you couldn't rape no slave. We was property, livestock, just like animals with numbers. Mama said she was thirteen when they came to the slave cabin saying the master needed a bed warmer and took her to his bed. When he got through using Mama, he fell asleep. She was so mad being used as a bed warmer she wanted to kill old master dead, right on the spot, but knew that hell and damnation would come down on the slaves if she did. So, instead she took this watch." She spit out juice again.

"It's the only thing of value she ever gave me, 'cept life of course, and my half-brother. That old buster got Mama pregnant that day. My half-brother was a house Nigger like most half-whites were, because the old masters didn't want their kids out in the fields picking cotton. They had it a little easier than most slaves, except the old masters' wives gave them hell 'cause most of the masters' and the slave women's kids look better than the masters' and their wives'

122

kids. They really were their half-brother or sisters." She rocked and took a sip.

"So they call them half-human, since they have half White blood in them. I often wonder how they can tell the 'good' White blood from the 'bad' Black blood?" She is laughing so loud, she almost knocks over her hot toddy.

"Be careful, Mrs. Peck, don't hurt yourself. Calm down and finish telling me the story."

"My son is on dope and my daughter is a drunk. Besides, they are old as dirt themselves. I'm gonna die in a day or two. I want you to have this. So, keep it to remember me by, and if you ever get in a jam...pawn it. Besides, I don't want no fancy preacher walkin' around showin' it off, or if it falls in the hands of some White man, I'll turn over in my grave. And that is what will happen when I am dead. So, hush up and take it!" She waved a frail hand at the watch.

"I heard you been up north going to school. Good for you, boy. You go back up there and make something out of yourself instead of hanging round here with these no good young folks drinking and taking that dope, stealing and acting like Niggers. That's the name the White man gave us 'cause he said we was lazy and shiftless. It didn't matter. He worked us from can't to can't—can't see in the morning till can't see at night. These young folks making him seem right. What the slave masters did to us, we're now doing to ourselves. Only worst, shooting and killing each other just like animals. We don't need the KKK any more to hunt us down and kill us like dogs. We are the new Black KKK and doing a better job of killing ourselves than they ever did." She spit again.

"I remember when I was a little girl. We was just Colored

then. Treated each other better, stuck together, helped one another out. If I had two pieces of bread, I'll give you one when we was Colored. Then we became Negroes and then just plain Blacks, then something called Afro-American. Now I think we call ourselves African American or who knows what?" A sip of toddy.

"It seems like ever time we change our name, we treat each other worse. We were better off when we were just plain Colored 'cause ain't none of us ever seen Africa. I may be black as tar, Son, you white as some White folks, and my daughter is copper color. So no matter what we call ourselves, we're still Colored. But, enough talk. Come give me a hug and say goodbye, 'cause I'm getting real tired. This is the last time you going to see me on this side of Jordan."

As I hold this old frail lady for the first time in my life, I understand what's meant by a person being more than just a body, because at that moment we are one in spirit. I know as sure as the River Heaven has been flowing for ever, so she would be in the real Heaven for ever. I try not to cry as I back away.

Mrs. Peck just smiles, "I am so happy," she says. "In a few days, I will be going home to glory, and may God bless you dear boy."

"Thanks for the watch Mrs. Peck. It's beautiful. It will always be dear to my heart. If I have to work two jobs I will never pawn it. I am on my way to a picnic down at the ballpark, but I will bring you some funny books later this evening, and a little Brown Mule."

"O my goodness, Son! You younger people don't know about the word picnic do you?" she asks.

"Well, before you go or I get out of breath, you must hear

why you should never use that damn word."

"What happened Mrs. Peck? Somebody get stung by a bee or ants go in someone's food or something? What's the reason you don't like the word picnic?"

"Son, I get angry every time I hear that word. When I was a little girl Mama use' to tell me about White folks and their Picnic. Pic means to pick a Black person to lynch and Nic was the White man's short name for Nigger. They shorten 'pick a Nigger' to 'picnic', and would have food, dance and make it a picnic as they lynch some poor Black slave. So tell our folk to use barbecue or outing, or make up a name, but never use picnic. Now go, Son, before I cross over into Jordan right in front of you. I am so weak and there is so much you don't know. Things the White folks keeps from you, but I am just too weak to tell you any more."

As I wave goodbye and walk away, I can't help from thinking of what Pops had said when he started teaching me, "History is best learned at the foot of an elder."

At 106 years old, and still in her right mind, with so much history and wisdom of the Colored people, all will be lost when Mrs. Peck goes. All the stories about her struggles, the whippings, then pouring salt in the wounds, the hardship our people had to deal with. The meaning of words like picnic will be lost to the next generation.

Maybe not, since she's been telling me these stories as far back as I can remember. Perhaps she means for me to become the story teller and that's why she gave me the watch to remind me.

Right now, all I can think about is how Mrs. Peck is so much different looking than Pops, like night and day, yet they are the same, very spiritual people. I also know now why Pops says the truth is universal and doesn't know color, race, or religion. The same can be said of a spiritual person.

35

Nina Simone

The next day is one of the biggest in the history of the Colored folks in Tryon. Fox is getting married and there will be a big party celebrating the closing of the Colored school.

Today, July third, 1966, Fox and Jolene are getting married at the Colored Baptist Church. Standing there as the best man, I watch Jade, and know for sure there's a God somewhere to make someone so beautiful. The long black silky hair against olive skin, a slim shapely body, exotic eyes, and a face even Lena Horne, the movie star, would envy. I want to marry her right on the spot.

After the wedding, we all head to the Colored school for the reception and the beginning of the party, celebrating the closing of the school later that night.

The school was named after Edmund Embury, a White man who gave the land and built the school many years ago. For a long time I thought the school was named after a Black man, but instead he was a good White man. Yet we still call it the Colored school.

Nina Simone's record of *I Love You Porgy* is playing as we enter. But soon a song called, *Let the Good Times Roll* starts playing. It's party time until around seven; then the program starts.

To my surprise, there are so many outstanding people from this little town: doctors, professors, undertakers and even an NBA player.

However, Nina Simone is the star and Tryon's most famous person. There is a rumor she might give a free concert tonight. Although Nina doesn't show, in some ways it turns out better.

Jolene plays the piano a lot like Nina, and Rebecca can sing almost like her. They practiced Nina's music just in case she doesn't come. They take their place at the piano.

"Before we perform some of Nina's songs," Rebecca says, "you older people remember her as Eunice Waymon when she used to run around here as a little girl. She now is a big time star. We want to tell you something about Eunice, excuse me, I mean our Nina. As y'all know, Nina is heavily involved in the Black movement. She so eloquently expresses her feelings when she sings *Mississippi Goddamn,* which is an angry response to the killing of Civil Rights advocate Medgar Evers, and the four little girls—Addie Mae Collins, Carole Robertson and Cynthia Wesley, all 14, and Denise McNair, 11, when a Ku Klux Klan bomb went off September 15, 1963 in Birmingham's Sixteenth Street Baptist Church in Alabama."

Then Jolene stands, "When Nina was ten," she says, "she was invited to give a concert at the Lanier Library. Mr. and Mrs. Waymon, her mother and father, came with her. Arriving early, they sat in the front row seats. However, as the White folks arrived, her parents were asked to stand in the back.

"Nina was devastated. Tryon has been both a blessing and a wound to Nina's soul. The citizens of Tryon made it possible for her to receive a fine musical education. Yet it's here her deep anger about racial discrimination was born."

"But God is good," Rebecca says, "and we don't have to

go to the back of nothing no more. And, as we close this school, let's say 'so long' to the old back-of-the-bus-Colored Uncle Tom ways, and hello-front-door, open wide, because here we come—Black, free and proud."

There is very loud and long applause along with some shouts of "Hallelujah!" and "Amen!" Mother Sunshine jumps up and hollers "Glory!" while beating her tambourine and shouting, "Thank you, Jesus!"

Rebecca begins playing fast Pentecostal shouting music and half the school is up shouting. Church is in session in the Colored schoolhouse. Head is grinning from ear to ear, as he points to Jade.

He says to me, "Your girlfriend sure looks funny, an Asian shouting to Black church music. I'll say one thing for her. She might be Asian but she sho' moves like a sister. She can sho' move her behind."

"Watch you mouth Head, 'fore I knock some of them BBs off you head, talking about my woman like that," I say.

After the people settle down, Rebecca continues, "The first song we do is sad, but very powerful. So sit back and try not to laugh at us as we imitate Nina."

They begin singing and playing *Strange Fruit,* a song about Black men hanging from tree. And definitely have the people's attention with *To be Young, Gifted and Black.*

"This is the Civil Rights Anthem, and our Nina is the leading singer of the movement," Rebecca says.

"Now we gonna change the mood with some of Nina's hot blues and jazz songs."

They play, sing, and have the school rocking. After a while, they stop to let the people catch their breath.

Jolene says, "If Nina could see us now, she would be so

proud of her little old home town. Husband," she calls. Motioning with her finger, she invites Fox up front to dance with her. But instead, when he gets there, Rebecca begins playing and Jolene sings Nina's hit called *I want a Little Sugar in My Bowl*. Then, she starts this sexy dance around him, swaying her body in sensual moves, even bumps up against him and grinds on him a little.

Rebecca says with a big smile, "Fox, look what you gonna get tonight. Hope you can handle it."

In a kidding voice, Jolene asks, while moving her hips, "Darlin' do you want to put a little sugar in my bowl?"

The audience goes wild with laughter.

Now it is our turn to put on our martial arts display. However, after Jolene and Rebecca's act, Fox turns to me.

"I wish we'd gone before them," he says. "They put on a hell of a show. It's a tough act to follow."

But we soon have the people oohing and aahing—breaking boards, and throwing each other around. At the end, I hand Fox a board telling him to hold it up over his head. I've tried this many times, but never have been able to leap up and break a board.

I look in the crowd and see Pops. He stands up. I look at him and he smiles and starts clapping, the people join him with a steady clap. I turn, concentrate and focus with all my might on the board. Then kick high into the air—and break the board.

I hit the floor and get up. The crowd is going wild, clapping and yelling. Fox and I look at each other like two gunslingers from the Old West and wonder who'd win if we really went at it.

Pops knew this day would come, but we would never

know because of our promise we made to him never to fight each other. I also know at this time Fox has Jolene and getting some is on his mind and he isn't about to waste time fighting.

The rest of the night is one big party with older people dancing, listening to Jimmie Reed singing the blues, and Louie Jordan swinging with music from the 'forties. Some James Brown and Little Richard are in the mix and the young people are really digging the older music.

Everyone is having fun until early in the morning. Grandma and Pops are out on the floor, but they get tired and leave early.

Fox comes up to me and says, "I am supposed to take sister home. Will you do it for me?" He doesn't wait for an answer. Jolene is busy talking to her girlfriends as Fox walks over and grabs her by the arm.

"Excuse me girls. Say goodnight to Jolene. She needs a little sugar in her bowl."

Jolene is still trying to talk to her girlfriends as she walks out the door.

"We all know where you are going. Don't do anything we wouldn't do," they kid her, throwing rice at them as they leave the school.

Then it is the last dance. A couple of the young boys go to Jade, but she walks over to me. Etta James starts singing *At Last*. We slowly dance, looking in each other's eyes. It's like a dream, as Etta sings, *At last my love has come along*. What a way to say goodbye to the Colored schoolhouse.

36

The End of an Era

After a lot of hugs and goodbyes, we leave the building. It's the end of an era, a Colored way of life. Integrating now into the White lifestyle and becoming a true American has to be a blessing and now our kids can get the same education as the Whites. All this is good.

However, losing the Colored way of life is not. Important aspects, such as the closeness of our own schools, our identity, our culture and history may be lost. Just like my other ancestors the American Indians. There may be no more colorful characters like Mother Shine, free to do her little dance without being laughed at, or called crazy. I think how sad this could be, but only time will tell.

As I walk Jade home in the warm Carolina night, we stop on the hill where Fox and I became blood brothers.

"Jade, this hill is my special place, my spot on earth where all is well. Let's sit and talk about our future."

"In two years, at eighteen, I want to marry you," she says. "Work a few years so we can buy a big house, then have lots of kids. What about you?"

"Jade, life without you is not life. So, tonight under the stars, if you say yes, we are engaged."

"I don't have to say yes, because you already have my heart, but, yes anyway, my love," she says.

We both want to lie down and kiss, but know if we do, we couldn't stop ourselves from doing it. I keep hearing in my head my promise to Pops. That damn Adam test of not getting any in the state of Carolina until I am eighteen.

Now I know why he made me make it: so I wouldn't do it to Jade. The old man is really smart. It is so hard not to make love to her, but my love, respect, and promise to him is the only thing stopping me.

Soon I walk her to her door. Before she enters, we kiss for a long time. My body is in tune with hers and even without getting some this is a great feeling, holding this Asian beauty so tight.

"Goodnight my love. I will see you in my dreams," Jade says, and she goes in. As I slowly walk back to my house, I am truly in love.

The next day is the Fourth of July. I am sitting in the swing on the porch when Fox and Jolene drive up.

Fox gets out of the car grinning from ear to ear. "Partner, I just want to say goodbye. We catch our plane for California in a short while. Also have to tell you it is well worth the wait. All those days she kept saying no, wait till we get married. Sometimes I hated her. Once or twice, I try to take it. I am truly a blessed man to have a woman of character like Jolene, and a blood brother like you."

We hug and Fox says, "Until our paths cross again, peace be with you best friend." He leaves with the smile still on his face.

With their departure, Tryon changed from this exciting spiritual park-like place to this small sleepy town. When they left, my heart and soul went with them, as if a part of me died.

As much as I love Tryon and it will always be my home, the city is now my home also. In a few weeks, I will be going back. However, today is a sleepy day as people sit, and some sleep, in the park after partying so hard at the schoolhouse. A few are playing cards, but most just lie around.

Mark is going back to the city tomorrow. Next week Sun is leaving to join this militant group up north, and Head is going to Morehouse, a Black college in Georgia. Soon all my buddies will be gone and it will just be Tryon and me. Then it hits me. I will have the beautiful Jade all to myself.

It is good food, good friends, and fireworks at night. It is a great Fourth of July; just as good as when we won the karate championship.

The bad news is one week later all my friends are gone; but the good news is Jade can use Pops' car.

It's late morning when Grandma says, "Come and get some breakfast, boy. You gonna sleep all day?"

Just then the phone rings.

"It's for you. It's that pretty girl with the good hair," Grandma says. I pick up the phone.

"Want to take a ride?" says Jade.

"Is an elephant big?" I say. "Let's ride."

We drive up into the mountains, park the vehicle, take out our fishing poles and hike through the woods down to a waterfall and sit on the bank. It's the same river that runs down to Tryon. The one we call Heaven.

"Jade, can you fish?" I ask.

"Better than you," she says, taking one of the poles and putting her own worm on the hook. After about an hour of fishing, "There is enough fish to eat," she says. "You clean them while I get the camp stove ready. There ain't nothing like eating fish right out of the water."

While sitting and eating, Jade teaches me a lot about

Buddhism and how the chanting keeps her calm and at peace, even helps her not to give in to me.

She says her body wants me so bad it hurts. I feel the same way so shortly I start chanting. Jade taught me a slow chant, "Om Mani Padme Hum." I like any and everything to help me keep that damn Adam test.

A most unusual thing happens as we sit on the bank. A squirrel is leaping through the trees jumping from one limb to another. This hawk is circling in the sky and keeps getting lower and lower. Then he swoops down, catching the squirrel in mid-air as it jumps from one limb to another. Jade lets out a little sigh and says, "What a sight. This will always be our special moment."

Almost all the rest of my daylight time in Tryon I spend with her. We canoe on the lakes, hike the mountain trails and sometimes take Pops and Doby with us. But soon it is time to head back up north.

Lucy comes down the last day before we are leaving. It is one of the hardest days of my life, even harder than the first time, because I love this place and the people. It seems like I am abandoning them, but they all want me to go, because they love me too, and know it is best for me.

Jade and I stay away from each other at night because it is too tempting and easy to make love in the dark. But my last night, I ask her to come to my spot on the hill.

We sit on a blanket and pledge our love for each other as we look up at all the stars, chant and say our goodbyes. As I slowly walk her home to her door, we kiss and hold each other for a long time.

"I love you with all my heart and will always be true to you," she says.

A quick kiss and she turns and goes inside.

As I walk away, I am crying and don't see Doby standing there until he makes a little whining sound. Then I sit down and pat him for a long time. Even he seems sad. After a while I go home, get ready to head for the city in the morning.

It has been a great summer.

37
Soaring

The ride back is long and sad. I have lots of time to think. I keep remembering Pops talking about how the eagle kicks its young out of the nest. They must fly or fall on the rocks below.

Tryon and childhood have been my nest where it is warm and safe. I want it to stay that way, but everyone has to leave that safe place and soar or crash on the rocks.

Fox is soaring and happy with Jolene, and Sun is off into his Black militant thing. Head is in college. Thinking about my buddies and them being happy helps, but my heart still aches for Jade.

A few days back in the city with so much to do, I am soaring myself. Then the air is let out of my sails when I get a letter from Fox saying he has been drafted, and is in Basic Training. I hope he doesn't go to Vietnam and get killed like Candy. I'm not sure I could take it if he did.

I don't have much time to worry about Fox because school begins. I am the starting quarterback on the football team and John is the wide receiver. We both are stars. Then from there we go into basketball; we both are stars. Then baseball is where I am the star and John runs track and is the star.

In the mostly White school, we are having the time of our lives because we are invited to all the house parties, both Black and White. Sometimes we are the only Blacks at some White parties and the White girls are all over us.

John is doing it to several different girls and wonders why I'm not. And so do I. At seventeen, my mind is always on getting some. I have a hard on when I go to bed, when I wake up and many times during the day.

Up until now, my love for Jade and promise to Pops, hold me back. They are so far away and who would know, I often think, but deep down I know it is almost like making a promise to God.

The sports, school, and winter time with ice and snow and no place to take a girl have helped me keep my promise. But now it's spring 1967 and the weather is warm. There's a house party on somewhere most weekends. I love dancing close with all these pretty girls. I have to get some soon.

All of a sudden it hits me like a ton of bricks. I remember Pops saying I could get some with one girl at seventeen, as long as it's out of Carolina. This girl named Vickie from school will be it. We talk in school all the time and even kissed once.

38
April Fool

I remember John telling me about the April Fools' Dance this Saturday. I call Vickie and ask if she is going.

"See you there," she says.

Now, I am a big boy.

When I walk in the party, Vickie has on this short tight red dress and high heeled shoes. With legs like Tina Turner, she is the finest thing in the party.

All the guys and some of the girls are looking at her when she comes over and speaks to me. We talk a while, then she dances with some other guys, but at the end of the party with the blue lights low we are together. As they play several slow jams, *In the Still of the Night*, by The Dells, we kiss and grind. She can really move her body.

When the music stops my pants are wet and I am hurting. Now I know what the blue balls are. I always thought the blue balls was a joke, but it's for real, and I have to get some soon.

I have my driving license now and Lucy's car is outside. So, I ask Vickie if we could go to Lover's Lane.

She smiles, "Maybe next week, if you want to be my boyfriend."

"I would love to, but can we go to the car now?"

"Next week," she says, as she leaves with her girlfriend.

It is April first and an April Fools' Dance. The joke is on me.

39
Finer Things in Life

Spreading my burlap sack to collect the refuse, I am singing *Searchin'*, by The Coasters, thinking about taking Vickie to Lover's Lane and looking forward to getting some at last. Then, as I got to the top, I see the Goddess waving at me to come and get some rubbish. I take it, tie up my sack and drop it into the courtyard,

"Do you want to come in and have a bite to eat?" she asks.

"Sure," I say, trying not to stutter.

As I enter the penthouse, I take off my shoes and walk into a *Style* magazine-type kitchen. Hanging plants, exotic painting, there is a romantic smell of incense in the air.

"Sit down at the table," she says. "I just made some corned beef and pastrami sandwiches with cherry cheesecake for dessert." She brings them over, sits down, and we begin to eat and talk.

"I have watched you over the years grow into a very well-built, good-looking young man. I've even been to several of your games. You are a magnificent athlete," she says.

"Thanks very much," I say, as I pinch myself to make sure I'm not dreaming, because it looks like the tall fine Goddess wants to give me some.

We get on the subject of art, culture, and music. She asks if I like symphony music.

"No, I am more into Little Richard, Chuck Berry, and R and B," I say.

"Let's go into the living room and I will educate you to some of the finer things in life," she says.

I walk into a room with cream-colored, deep pile carpet and a white bearskin rug lying in front of a real wood-burning fireplace.

"This is like something out of *Home and Garden* magazine," I say.

"Take this very fine cabernet wine. Drink it slowly while you listen to one of my favorite symphonies called Rachmaninoff piano concerto number two.

"Relax, and listen to the different instruments as they rise and fall. Try and pick out each one, the piano, strings, and so forth," she says, as the music plays. Then, "Let's sit on the couch."

We do and the sound of the music is all around us.

"Wow, I didn't realize what I've been missing not listening to such great music," I say.

Since I very seldom drink, the wine has me feeling warm and mellow. I can't keep my eyes off her shapely creamy white thighs, as her short white robe is slightly open, showing her long legs.

Her head tilts slightly back and her eyes close, listening to the music. Her chest rises and falls slowly as she takes deep breaths letting them out slowly. I just have to try and kiss her. As I do, she doesn't stop me. Instead she puts her tongue in my mouth and kisses back hard. I start to climb on top of her, but she stops me.

"Easy, easy. Making love is like a symphony that starts off slow and builds to a climax like the Rachmaninoff concerto. The slower you go, the longer you will last."

Then she takes my hand and leads me to the bedroom and

takes off her robe. She doesn't have on any panties and seems very proud of her well proportioned body. Her robe barely hits the floor before I have my clothes off. She walks over and kisses me. I feel her breasts pressing against my chest, and a slow grind against my hard-on.

Then we lie on the bed, kissing. I slowly roll on top of her and as I enter her she says, "Slow…slow," and starts moving her body to the sound of Rachmaninoff.

Shortly I feel like someone is tickling my behind with a feather and I hear funny noises in the room. Then I realize it's me making them, and a joy that I have never felt before comes over me. All the frustrating times I suffer because of that damn Adam test is finally coming to an end. I push hard and have my first climax. She arches her back and goes limp for a moment.

I wonder if I seriously hurt the Goddess by putting my entire thing in her. But when I look at her face she has a beautiful smile and so do I. I roll over and think if only Fox, Sun, John, Markey or some of the boys could see me now. Thank God for Rachmaninoff.

We make love several more times that day and she is right. She does educate me in the finer things in life, good wine, symphony music, but ain't nothing finer than getting some.

40

Vickie

The phone rings. It's Vickie. "Well, ballplayer, today's the day we have a date. You forget?"

"No. I'll pick you up in a short while."

We go to see a movie. When we come out we stop to have a hot dog and soda. We sit around talking about college, and what we plan to do after high school.

"It's so crowded and loud in here. Let's take a ride in the park where it's quiet and we can talk," Vickie says.

"Sounds good," I say.

I knew this is a way of saying let's go to Lover's Lane. As we pull into this real dark place with no one around, I know my Adam test is in trouble.

As we hug and kiss, my mind knows better, but my body is weak. This is the eternal battle between body and soul, the test to see if you control your body or it you. My body is winning.

Life's strong desire for sex is a personal battle between good and evil, a test of one's spirit and character. My body is burning with desire, a natural strong magnet, pulling me to this beautiful young woman, and to my thing there is no such thing as evil.

But your spirit, the part that is supposed to separate you from an animal, is what Pops told us over and over is so hard to overcome. I made a promise to this old man in Tryon, and if I hit this hot young lady, he would never know. But, I would. If only I hadn't done it to the Goddess, I could make love to this fine Vickie. However, my word of only one woman until eighteen, that damn Adam test is like a promise to God, which the perfect man, Adam himself, even lost. So, how could I overcome my problem with this hot Vickie?

I jump up, get out of the car, lean against it, and start chanting, "Nam-Myoho-Renge-Ky, Nam-Myoho-Renge-Kyo," over and over again. It's another Buddhist Chant Jade and I used to do. My thing is hard and sticking straight out of my pants when Vickie gets out of the car.

She says in a loud voice, "All the boys are chasing me, wanting to buy me nice things and I end up with a crazy nut like you. I have never had sex, and you could have been my first, but you just blow your chance. Put your thing back in your pants and take me home."

She looks at me and just falls out laughing so hard she could barely say, "Take me home, please."

As we drive home, it is long and silent. Then I tell her of my Adam test. How, despite of wanting her so badly, it hurts, I made a promise to be celibate until eighteen. "Maybe you can understand if I told you it is a part of my martial arts code."

Vickie laughs out of control.

"You were so funny out there in the dark with your thing out, chanting. I thought you were losing your mind," she says. "We can be friends without doing it. As I just said, I haven't done it yet. Besides you will be eighteen soon. Then, I will screw your brains out. You know I am glad for your Adam test thing, because I would have kind of hated to lose my virginity in the back seat of a car. Although at the time I was good and ready. Let me out here. It's about two blocks from my house. I need to walk a little to cool off."

I stop. She opens the door and says, "I really had a nice time. Call me later."

I watch her walk down the street, prancing like a young Kentucky filly. I think what a beautiful sight and I ask myself was it really the Adam test that kept me from making love to her or was it my love for Jade?

Other than not being able to get some from Vickie, it was a great summer.

41
Sun's Letters

In early August, Sun's letter arrives. His first one came in January and we started writing each other monthly.

Sun always begins with "I have some good news and some bad."

In January, the good news was on the third. Jack Ruby walked right up to Lee Harvey Oswald (the man who killed President Kennedy) and blew him away. The bad news was that damn segregationist Lester Maddox became governor of Georgia. Why didn't Black folks use their vote...and all the good White folks? They know to vote that prejudiced SOB out of office. "Negroes gonna still catch hell down there."

In April, he wrote about our good brother Muhammad Ali refusing military service, telling the Army he didn't have a fight with the Viet Cong. "Ain't none of them ever called me no 'Nigger'." The bad news was they took his boxing license away. Who knows how long before we'll see the greatest 'flow like a butterfly and sting like a bee' again?

In May, I answered his letter telling him we lost Langston Hughes, one of our greatest Black writers and my favorite. Langston wrote a great play called *Raisin in the Sun*. A few lines from one of his poems I learned in the Colored School in Tryon called *Cross* about a person of mixed race. Being one myself, it has stayed with me until this day. It reads:

My old man died in a fine big house
My Ma died in a shack

I wonder where I'm gonna die,
Being neither White or Black
Another one I don't remember the name, but the few
lines are some I live by:
Happiness lives nowhere,
Some old folk said,
If not within oneself.
Sun's next letter comes late this August evening, telling
me about what happened in July—almost all bad news. It
starts out with the great saxophone John Coltrane dying at
the age of 41. Coltrane's jazz is a little bit too far out for me,
but being born in North Carolina same as me, he was still
my man.

Sun then writes about all the riots he has been to in the
last few weeks. On July 13th, there was a race riot in New
Jersey. But the one that changed his way of thinking was the
one in Detroit on the 23rd.

Twelfth Street, in a predominantly Black inner city
neighborhood, had one of the worst race riots in United
States history. In five days, 43 people died; 342 were injured
and 1,400 buildings burned. Sun wrote:

In the beginning, this was thrilling, a Black revolu-
tion. We were showing the White man he couldn't treat
us like slaves any more.

You know me and how I hate the White man. My
hero has always been people like Stokely Carmichael
who coined the phrase 'Black Power', Malcolm X's
slogan of 'By any means necessary,' Nina singing
Mississippi Goddamn *or James singing* I'm Black and
I'm proud. *You know me, anything Black and militant.*

When I was 16, I believed all that because I was

ignorant. My favorite saying, as you know is, 'Ignorance is bliss'. But I am 20 now and no longer ignorant. Maybe it was bliss when the south was still segregated, sometimes you looked the other way, and might even say 'yesa boss', just to keep your sanity. But now with all the new opportunities open up for us, there is no excuse being ignorant, and it certainly is not bliss.

After all the killing and burning were over, I realized Dr. King is right. Now I have new heroes like Gandhi in India who changed India through non-violent means. My greatest or I should say our greatest hero is Dr. King. King's peaceful 'We shall overcome' way is the only way to help our people better themselves. It got us the right to vote, ended segregation and made us true Americans.

Burning down cities and killing people is not what we should be about. Going to school, starting businesses, making this country better for all people because, like it or not Black or White, we are all in the same boat. I am beginning to sound like Dr. King, my friend [smile], so I had better close. I am going to Tryon in September, so maybe we can meet. Please let me know. Until then I'm off to another race riot. Just kidding!

As always,

Sun.

The rest of the summer goes fast, with pick-up basketball games in the day with college players and other rough older players. Almost every day I play against a small college All-American and hold my own. My game improves tremendously. Labor Day comes too soon, signaling the closing of the swimming pool, parks, and all the good summer fun things and the start of school and shortly cold weather. I am enjoying it all. I am a senior now and having the time of my life. I am the star and captain of both the basketball and football teams. I make All State in both. I am treated like a Rock star everywhere I go. Life is great. Thanksgiving, Christmas and New Year, are so much fun; the cold weather is almost invisible, and I even enjoy the snow.

It's Spring now and the city even has the nerve to have some warm spring weather, with flowers. My baseball coach asks me to go talk to one of his buddies about college. So I go.

42
A King Is Lost

April 4, 1968. A little after six pm, I am in this expensive restaurant eating a big steak dinner and talking to my baseball college coach about going to his college.

"Can I have everyone's attention please?" A well-dressed man, maybe the manager, says, "I have some terrible news."

He pauses a second to let the people stop talking, so everyone can hear. A few didn't pay him any attention, so he took a big spoon and beat on a big pot. When he had everyone's attention he says in a quivering voice.

"I don't know any easy way to say this, so I'll just come out and say it. Martin Luther King Jr. has just been shot on the balcony of the Lorraine Hotel in Memphis."

There is a moment of silence when everyone freezes in disbelief. I will always remember where I was when I hear this terrible news. Almost everyone pays their bill and leaves. Both Blacks and Whites are crying. Color doesn't seem to matter. We leave and already I can hear sirens in the street. The first thing that comes to my mind is whether there will be more riots like Detroit last year and the Watts riots in 1965 out in L.A. I hope that because King preached non-violence, this will help keep the lid on the city. I remember him talking about riots when he said, "A riot is the language of the unheard." People are praying King will live, but shortly the bad news comes. He doesn't make it.

I hurry home, and the next three days my worst fear comes to pass. Over a thousand fires are reported in

Washington, D.C. King's death leads to riots in more than 100 cities, and the riots don't stop until the 14th. Even the baseball season is postponed. No one knows how many people the authorities kill as they try to suppress the rebellion. The news says 46 people died; 41 of them Black including fourteen teenagers. This is the greatest rebellion in modern U.S. history. It's sad to say, but his death has made America a war zone, but his funeral brings America closer together, making us realize we are all Americans and this fighting really is against ourselves.

By June first, the city is healed somewhat from King's assassination. It is starting off as the best week of my life. I just signed a big contract to play Major League baseball. It is not an easy decision because I have full scholarships to most of the major colleges. However, the signing bonus is just too much money to say no to. Now I can buy Aunt and Uncle a nice house and get them out of that caretaker job. Mark shows me how and where to invest in the stock market, so if I don't splurge too much, I am set for life.

All this is good, but what really had me smiling and so happy is I am eighteen and that damn Adam test is over. Vickie and I are going to see James Brown Saturday night, then go on to a hotel. The next week I am taking the homecoming queen from another school to her prom, then to a hotel.

I am going to have big fun making up for that Adam test.

43
Surprise

A surge of happiness flows through my body like ice-cold lemonade on a hot day. I am getting ready to go to the basketball court when the Goddess calls asking me to come up; she has something real important to tell me. Her voice on the phone is shaky sounding like she is about to cry. This only makes her voice more sexy. I can hardly say, "Be right there." Quickly up the fire escape I run. She has the door slightly open. Entering I already have a hard on.

"Glad to see you. Come and give me a big hug," she says. "I have cooked you dinner, so set down and eat and make sure you drink your wine."

I sit down at the table with some of the most succulent food I ever had.

"Let's eat and drink slowly, talk, enjoy, and when we finish I have something to tell you, if you promise not to interrupt me," she says.

"Okay, if that's what you want, but can we go lie down and make a little love before you talk?" I ask.

"No, not today, my love. After my talk you might not want to anyway. Besides this is something you would never imagine in a thousand years that I'm going to tell you."

"Oh, I'll still want to lie down with you, even if I only had a day to live. Whatever you tell me ain't gonna stop me from eating this great food, besides you have me curious, so please go head and tell me."

"As you wish," she says. "Do not stop me because this is hard for me to say, and once I start please let me finish. Okay?"

"Sure, love, I am all ears. Besides, after drinking almost half a bottle of this fine cabernet the sound of your voice is music to my ears."

"I love two men, but in different ways. You, I love totally with all my heart and soul. Making love with you sets my body on fire and I miss you when we are apart. I'm not sure you know, but I am married. My husband is very rich, much older than me, and is well known but is impotent. He can't make a baby," she smiles sadly.

"One night we went to see a movie called *The Barefoot Contessa,* where a women, played by Ava Gardner, got pregnant by another man because her husband was impotent, she did it for him because he wanted a child of his own so bad. That is where I got the idea. Please don't be angry, I watched you with your great body, great in sports, and picked you to get me pregnant. You did, and you have a son."

"This is a joke. Right?" I say. "How do you know it's mine?"

As I look at her, tears come to her eyes.

"You hurt my feelings, I am not a tramp, and besides I've only slept with two men in my life, you and my husband. I didn't know I would fall in love with you. It was not in my plan, but I love you. Take a look at this picture—this is your son."

He is the spitting image of me.

"What a sharp little boy. You are right I don't want any more food or sex, but I can use a big glass of wine. I am in total shock, but kind of happy at the same time, I've only been to bed with one woman and me a father at eighteen, hard for me to believe."

"War, I picked you to be the father, you don't have to worry about support and you can see him very soon."

"You're crying. Don't cry, it's Okay. Come and let me hold you," I say.

We embrace for a long time and, as I hold her tight, she starts breathing hard. I open her robe and feel her breasts against my chest. She doesn't stop me when I pull her panties down and start to enter her. She makes a soft moaning sound.

"Wait," she says. "You are so bad," as she heads for the bedroom.

I am right behind her. Near the bed she turns and kisses me hard, while her breathing is fast like she just ran a mile. We lie on the bed. She makes me get on my back, and she climbs on top of me. Up and down she moves her body like a belly dancer as she gives me the ride of my life.

After we finish making love, she lies with her head on my chest. I think to myself whoever said 'nothing can be finer than being in Carolina in the morning' lied. Being in the arms of the Goddess once again is much finer.

Hours later with a heavy heart I say goodbye to the fabulous Goddess and head for the swimming pool to cool off.

After making love to the Goddess I feel totally relaxed like I am walking on air. I almost don't see the little kid kick his ball and it is rolling into the street; his mother is talking to some lady as the kid starts for the ball.

I see this car headed straight for him. I holler at the kid, but he doesn't stop.

In that split second as I look at the kid, I think he might

grow up to be the next Einstein...or the next Hitler. Someone who could cure cancer...or be a serial killer and the world would be better off if he died now. But if I don't act soon he'll be dead. Without thinking my instincts take over.

I run, dive tackling the kid, and drag him back on the sidewalk to safety.

44

Hero

I think I made it until I feel the pain like someone has my leg in a vise, squeezing it tighter and tighter. I have been hit hard in football and karate, but never experienced pain like this. As I lie there I can hear people crying and talking. Shortly I hear a siren off in the distance. I find myself beside this river called Heaven deep in the Carolina woods and I'm at peace as I dive into darkness.

Days later I wake up in a hospital room. Looking around, my leg is bandaged up like an Egyptian mummy. Over to my right two nurses are crying. A light is shining above my leg and I think I have died and am having an out-of-body experience, looking down on my own body. I read where you see this bright light just before you pass over into the other world.

But the light is a television set. Glancing up at it, there's a funeral in process. I hear the nurses crying and for a moment think it's mine. As my head clears from all the drugs, I can see it is a Kennedy. I think it is a rerun of President John Kennedy's assassination; except this is live television. I am confused, so I call a nurse over and ask what's going on.

"Sorry to tell you this," she says with teary eyes. "But Bobby Kennedy, the President's brother was shot and killed in California while you were sleeping."

"But. nurse, it was only two months ago Martin Luther King was assassinated," I say. "What is becoming of our country assassinating such great leaders? I feel sorry for our country. Since the passing of the Civil Rights Act it's gone crazy." This is so sad I momentarily forget about my leg.

As I watch the beautiful riderless black stallion prancing in the funeral procession like a high-spirited Arabian, the doctor appears and I don't like the look on his face. It looks like news I don't want to hear.

"Hello, how is my hero today?" the doctor asks.

"I don't feel much pain, but can't move my leg."

"Son, I'm just going to come right out and tell you. Because you are so young and strong, with so much muscle, we were able to save your leg. Unfortunately you can never play pro sports."

With this news, and Kennedy's funeral, I begin to cry. This is like my own death. I have trained my whole life to be an athlete. Competitive training such as lifting weights, running up hills, and learning martial arts are a way of life. Now what will life be without sports? I feel myself getting really depressed and try to get up. The doctor gives me a shot. As I drift off to sleep, I can feel the tears running down my cheeks.

Over the next few days I begin to feel a little better. The kid I saved and his mother come in, hugging me and thanking me for saving his life.

"Please, come to dinner when you get well and please be my son's godfather," she says. "If there is anything you need or want please call me, any time of the night, just call and it's yours."

"Sure, I would love to be his godfather. Me and your son will never forget each other." She kisses me softly on my check, whispers in my ear, "Thanks again," and leaves crying.

The man whose car hit me comes in.

"I saw the kid at the last moment and put on my brakes too late. My insurance will take care of everything, so relax and get well soon. You did a great thing saving that child's life."

He says goodbye. As he walks out the door I see him start to cry. With all my athlete friends, people from school and everyone calling me a hero, it helps ease my pain. I just wish they would stop crying when they leave.

Vickie arrives and reality hits me. I will not be going to a hotel with her any time soon. There will be no playing ball in the big stadiums or even taking her to our high school prom. All I have to look forward to is this horrible pain in my leg.

Vickie comes over, kisses me on the cheek and, with a soft sexy voice in my ear, says, "Darling, you are young and strong, and in a few months you'll be back to your old self. When that happens I have something for you to make you feel 'real good.'" She shakes her hips in a suggestive way. "Meanwhile, anything you want or need, just call on me."

She sits and talks with me a long time. Then leaves crying.

The doctor comes in.

"Time to get up and learn to use crutches, and if you learn quick and promise to take your pain medicine, you might be able to go home next week."

The nurse shows me how to use crutches, and as soon as she gives them to me I walk slowly to the bathroom. In spite of my pain it feels good just to do that. A few days later the doctor gives me lots of pain pills, a schedule for my treatment, and tells me I can go home.

45

Depressed and Angry

As they roll me out of the hospital I look up. The shining sun feels so good I almost forget I am in a wheelchair and will be using crutches for a long time.

The next few months are pure hell. With rehabilitation, sitting down and not being able to move much, my whole lifestyle has changed. For the first time I am becoming depressed and angry. At eighteen, how could this happen to me? I keep telling myself I saved a little boy's life, but was it worth it, giving up the best part of mine?

It's November and although rehab has been hell, now at last I can walk slowly using a cane. It starts to snow—seems early this year. The thought of slipping in bad weather, and maybe setting my rehab back, makes me want to go south, back to Tryon and my roots. Now I hate the city. It has killed Martin Luther King, the Kennedy brothers, and Malcolm X, and made me a cripple.

The hospital forwards my medical records to Tryon. Mark drives me to the airport. He has been a true friend all through this ordeal. Driving me back and forth from the doctors and hospital. I owe him. However, his favorite saying is, "Friends don't keep score."

I am walking with a cane. As I get my ticket they push me in a wheelchair aboard the plane. They let me go first. This is killing my pride. I am used to being strong. Now I feel like an old man. I walk so slowly even Grandma could beat me in a race.

I return to Tryon not as a champion, but a young old man. When I move too fast, the pain hits like a hot poker. I am almost ashamed to go home, but maybe the peace of the Blue Ridge Mountains in the fall with all the golden falling leaves can lift my spirits.

It is almost Thanksgiving. From the air I can see snow on the ground. We arrive at the Greenville-Spartanburg Airport. Upon exiting the plane, the air is warm, in the seventies with a gentle breeze. Already the warm weather has me feeling better.

They put me in a wheelchair again. For the first time in months I don't feel sorry for myself. Beside me is a soldier in a wheelchair with one leg. His buddy beside him has only one arm. They lost their limbs fighting in the Vietnam War. I feel ashamed sitting in the wheelchair. I can feel their eyes looking at me funny. The one-legged one leans over and ask me in a sarcastic voice, "What's wrong with you boy? Got a pulled muscle, a hangnail or something?"

He says it in a way that makes me feel small, like I am a fake or something.

"No. I broke my leg in several places, dove in front of a speeding car and saved a little boy's life. Otherwise I would've gone to Nam like you. I am a small hero, not a real hero like you, fighting for our country, putting your life on the line. You are a true hero."

He looks at me and the expression on his face changes like he wants to cry. I can see the joy in his eyes. My words make him feel proud.

"Thanks for the kind words. Hope you get better soon." He pushes away in his chair with a smile, while his one-armed buddy walks beside him.

Watching him, I feel good for what I said to him. Since I hurt so much myself, I almost let my anger hurt that poor kid's feeling. Without Pops' training to think of the other person before you speak, I wanted to ask him how did you get hurt killing and blowing up people in their own homeland? But I think no telling what horror he went through in that terrible war in Vietnam. Now I am double sad, a bad leg and feeling sorry for the two young men who lost an arm and leg fighting for my freedom.

It is about twenty-five miles to Tryon. As I leave the airport building, I am expecting the Colored taxi driver to pick me up. To my surprise there is Grandma, Pops, and Jade. She's home from college for Thanksgiving.

Jade is no longer a girl, but a young beautiful woman at eighteen. Seeing her lifts my spirits for a moment, making me forget all the hurt and pain over the last several months. Without thinking, we fall into each other's arms, kissing and forgetting there are other people around.

Pops pulls us apart.

"Enough of that," he says, with a little smile and hugs me. The ride to Tryon is uplifting. Laughing and talking with the people I love brings much joy.

Pops pulls up to our house. We say our goodbyes and as he leaves he says, "See you for lunch tomorrow."

Pops never raises his voice or explains a lot of things. Fox and I always do whatever he says. I know I will be at his house for lunch tomorrow.

After a good night's sleep I wake up refreshed. I sit on the front porch in the swing, talking to Grandma. People who are walking by stop to talk and welcome me home. One nice thing about a small town is that everybody knows everybody. It feels good talking to them. I know I'm home when Mother Sunshine comes by and hollers "Glory," beats her tambourine and does her little sanctified dance for me.

At lunchtime I drive Grandma's car down to Pops'. As I enter the gate with my cane, Doby comes from around the house growling, not recognizing me. I call his name, "Doby! Doby!" His tail wags. He comes over and I hug and pet him like a long lost friend.

Pops comes out with the big stick he always carries, the one I have dodged many times in the Dojo. With one single blow he breaks my cane in half. I am stunned. What will I do without my cane? I certainly can't say anything to him.

"Come on, let's go in the house. Lunch is ready," he says.

I hop on my good right leg to the table where we talk and eat lunch. After lunch, Pops puts my leg in this funky smelling hot water.

"Let it soak," he says.

Later he rubs some awful stuff that smells just as bad on my leg, then tells me to come back tomorrow. I leave, and for the first time in months I walk without crutches or a cane. My leg feels heavy like it weighs a ton—very stiff with just a little pain as I make it to the car. I drive home, get my pain medicine then take a nap.

46
God's Greatest Gift

In a dream-like state I hear Grandma calling, "Someone here to see you," she says.

"Ma, I don't feel like getting up. Tell them to come on in or come back later."

"Boy get up out of that bed, ain't gonna tell you no more. Besides, it's that pretty foreign girl with that good hair. Bet you get up now."

Half asleep I stagger to the door, open it and wake up real fast. Standing there in a real short red dress, high heel shoes, with her long black hair blowing in the breeze, and a little smile on her face, is Jade.

"Come on in. You just in time for supper. There's plenty," Grandma says from the kitchen. I go wash up and get dressed quickly.

We eat and talk with Grandma a while, then leave to go to town to a new so-called 'Jazz Club', with no one playing. But some real mellow jazz plays through the speakers.

"Isn't it nice to have a club that's just a club without being Colored or White?" Jade says, as she drinks a Virgin—no alcohol—drink. We make small talk, as we look in each other eyes. Jade says, "It's getting dark, let's take a ride."

We drive over to my favorite place in the whole world, the spot up on the hill where Fox and I became blood brothers.

Jade and I lay and talked here many times before. But as

163

she spread the blanket we both sense this is different. Now there is no Adam test to stop us, we are eighteen and adults. Without a word we kiss and even this is different, for it is a passionate kiss that sends pleasure all through my body. So many times we have held back, but not with this kiss.

As we lie there kissing, she is breathing hard and doesn't stop me when I undo her blouse and play with her breasts. They are hard and firm like some artist has made them perfect, not too big or too small, but perfect. She pushes me away just long enough to take off her panties.

"This is my first time. I've been ready to give myself to you for so long. This is a perfect place on this hill, our favorite spot, at night under the stars with the person I love with all my heart. Kiss me again, my darling, and let nature take her course," Jade says as she lies on top of me. Kissing me hard she guides me into her and this becomes the best day of my life.

The many times we had kissed, and held each other close was a warm sensual feeling, but nothing compared to feeling her body move in perfect rhythm under me, and hear her whisper my name softly saying, "I love you."

We make love off and on the rest of the night, under the stars like the Indians used to do—and many other people, before everything got so crowded. Luckily there is still a spot in Tryon where, at night you can look around and see no people. Just us, looking up at the stars shining like a million diamonds in the night. We fall asleep in each other arms.

When morning comes we both know we are in love. We talk of getting married, but Jade wants to finish college first, if we can wait that long. As we walk back to the car my leg feels much better. I can now walk without my cane and my spirits are as high as my love for Jade. Making love to her is a spiritual experience and I have just been to Heaven. Not God's house, or the river in the woods, but in the arms of God's greatest gift to man.

47
King Richard

I sit in the swing on the porch listening to bluejays singing loudly in the tall oak tree, as if singing praise to the Creator for making such a beautiful day.

Grandma opens the door and says, "I've cooked lots of food. I have a fresh turkey with cornbread stuffing, sweet potatoes and collard greens, right out of the garden, apple pie with apples off our tree, and a little home-made apple cider to drink after dinner. I want this day to be just you and me. You spend enough time with your hoodlum friends ripping and running, but today is ours."

It turns out great, just me and her eating so much we can barely move, and reflecting on our blessings.

Later that evening, I get a call from Jade to come down for dessert. My stomach is so full I don't want to move, but I know she wants to see me, and Grandma has eaten so much she's sleepy anyway. So I go down. We sit around the table talking, eating home-made apple pie and ice cream. Pops comes in and joins us.

"Good news. Got a letter from Fox. He is getting out in two months. He is one of the lucky ones that didn't go to Vietnam. Jade, get me a big dish of vanilla ice cream," he says, while reading the sports section of the newspaper.

"You know, I've never been to Charlotte to see the city and tomorrow my hero, Richard Petty, is racing. One of these days I'm going to take me a vacation and go see old Richard race."

We sit and chat a while. I say, "Goodnight y'all. This is a nice way to end Thanksgiving, but after so much food I got to go home and take a nap."

Jade walks me to the door and tells me of her plan for tomorrow. "Sounds good," I say. "See you then."

As I slowly walk home, I am happy and full.

The following day Jade and I tell Pops we have a surprise for him.

"Good! I like surprises! What is it?" he asks.

"We can't tell you, then it wouldn't be a surprise. It's such a nice day. Let's take a ride," Jade says.

We put him in the back seat of the car and start driving. He keeps asking, but we don't tell him where we are going. After a couple of hours of driving, I look in the back seat and find Pops asleep. I look out the window. Some way ahead the road sign says Charlotte 20 miles.

"Wake up, Pops!" I holler.

Pops jumps up looking around, saying, "Did you see that sign? It says Charlotte ain't but 20 miles."

I laugh, "Pops! Are you surprised? You're supposed to be so smart. It took you all this time to figure out we are taking you to see the big city."

"Yeah, Pops," Jade says, "and for all the things you have done for us, raising us right, lots of times doing without, just so we could have nice things, and teaching my big strong boyfriend martial arts. We can never repay you, and we realize you did it out of love. But guess what? We can do something very special for you. Come on? Guess what it is!"

"I give up. Come on! Quit playing with me! What are you two up to?"

"Pops! Does the name 'King' mean anything to you? And

167

I don't mean Elvis Presley."

"The King in North Carolina is Richard Petty, not some hip-shaking hillbilly from Tennessee, trying to sing like he's Black! Although the boy is pretty good. But go on...tell me about the real King!"

"Well, Pops, we just happen to have three tickets to see him race today, unless you would rather go downtown and shop around."

"Don't y'all kid me about the King! This ain't no joking matter," Pops says.

"This is no joke, Pops! Here they are," says Jade, holding up the tickets. "We ought to be at the track in a short time."

"Hallelujah! Looks like I did raise you right, child. Praise the Lord! Y'all are going to make an old man shout like Mother Sunshine on a Sunday morning."

I can't wipe the smile off my face, because it gives me great joy to see this grand old man, who taught me martial arts and how to live a good life, jumping around, screaming like a little kid as the King wins the race by a car length. After the race we tour the city taking in the sights.

We take Pops to a fancy steakhouse. He almost faints when he sees the price of a steak. We have to force him to stay because he says he could buy half a cow for that price. But no matter where we go or what we do, we never can stop Pops from talking about that race.

48
Chimney Rock

I wrap my best sweater with my school letter on it and give the package to Jade. I tell her not to open it until she gets to college.

She's already packed all her school gear, loaded her car, and said her goodbyes to all her friends, because this is going to be our day.

We drive up the mountains to Chimney Rock Park, only a short drive from Tryon. We take the unique elevator inside the rock twenty-six stories to the top, walk out on the edge of the rock, and stand in awe of the panoramic view. It takes my breath away to see the 1200 vertical feet down, along Hickory Nut Gorge to Lake Lure. We can see King's Mountain seventy-five miles away.

We hike the mountain's forest trails, uncrowded now since the leaves are about gone, to the majestic Hickory Nut Falls with a sheer drop of 404 feet. The waterfall is one of the highest in eastern America.

"You know we are so lucky to be born in this part of Carolina. Where else can you see such natural beauty? All this hiking has made me exhausted! Let's go find us a place to sleep," Jade says.

A short ride down from the rock is a motel sitting right on this picturesque mountain stream, with the water running right by the rooms. We check in and sit on the front porch listening to the sound of water cascading off the rocks as it flows by.

"Isn't it great how the South has changed? Just a few years ago we couldn't stay in this motel because of our color. Now the only color that counts is green," Jade says.

As we sit on the porch talking, a strong wind begins to blow.

"Storm acomin'," I say.

The ground is covered with leaves with only a few left in the trees; the wind blows them in the air circling all around us. It's like being in a magical leaf storm. For a long time we sit there watching the leaves flying to and fro like small magic carpets.

"Jade, just think, a few weeks ago the leaves were full of lush colors of burnt orange and fiery reds. The Creator had made a masterpiece of fall colors all over the area. A painting Michelangelo or any other human can't touch. People from all over the States drive down to see the magnificent fall foliage in its glorious splendor. Now leaves are just a rusty brown ground covering."

"Oh darling, you describe the fall color like a poet, come give me a big hug. You have my body tingling with excitement," she says.

The rain starts to fall, softly at first, just a light mist, and then slowly turns into a hard downpour. A 'gully washer,' as Grandma calls it, reverberating in the trees, forcing the remaining leaves to the ground. The sounds of nature are all around us.

"This is so romantic with the sound of the stream, the rain and the wind," Jade says. "Let's go in and get under the covers, it's cooling off and I'm chilly."

I smile because I know she is hot, not chilly.

We go inside; I sit on the bed and watch as she slowly

takes off her blouse. Wiggles out of her shorts and takes off her bra. The world's best artist could never do justice to her perfectly formed breasts. The room is almost dark as she removes her panties. A lightning flash briefly shows me her shapely body, creating an image that will be burned in my brain for eternity.

"I'm neckid and you still have your clothes on. Something wrong?" she asks.

"Nothing wrong, darling, just stunned by your beauty. This is a moment in time I want to remember for the rest of my life. When someone asks what was the best day of your life I will say the night I spent in the storm with you, my soul mate, the one that makes me complete."

I hurriedly take off my clothes and get into bed. I hold her close to me, running my hand over the warm smooth curves of her tight body. Our lips meet in a soft, tender kiss, and like a magnet our bodies join together in perfect harmony. With the thunder booming and lightning flashing through the open window, I feel like we are one with nature.

After making love for a long time I have the most peaceful satisfying sleep in my life. Some time later Jade wakes me.

"I'm hungry," she says.

We move slowly in a dream-like state, dress and drive to a nearby restaurant. We eat fresh mountain trout, fried okra, string beans, sweetened tea, with blackberry cobbler for dessert.

Back at the motel we spend the night talking and making love, while listening to the sounds of nature all around us.

49

Jade Leaves

Jade pats Doby for a long time as he whines, almost sounding like he's saying goodbye.

Tearfully she turns and hugs Pops, kisses him on the cheek.

"I love you and will miss you."

She hugs me tight for a long time and whispers in my ear, "Don't cry, my darling, I will cry enough for both of us. I'll have the memory of this week, especially last night, to help me make it through this semester. You will be the last thing I see before I sleep at night."

She goes without looking back, and gets in her car, weeping.

Watching her drive away is very hard, like watching happiness fade into the distance. Going in to face Pops for lunch and my treatment on my leg is almost as hard.

I have no idea what he will do to me. Although Jade is eighteen and grown, even though we are engaged to be married in July, she still is his little girl, and I know he knows we have done it.

There is no lunch on the table. Pops asks me to come into his room. I am thinking he's going to kill me. Instead he shows me his CB radio and his overseas ham radio.

"These are my hobbies."

He turns on the CB and talks to the truckers. Lots of them know him. They all have nicknames—just like Sun, Fox, Head and me. Except they call their nicknames handles.

Pops' handle is Pops, and as he goes through the channels, he comes across a gay channel.

We listen as one calls himself Ben Gay; another is Ramrod and there's Loose Booty. But my favorite one is Black, and calls himself Brown Sugar. He says, "Sweetie you be nice and Brown Sugar will give you some cake tonight."

The way they talk in a high-pitched feminine voice with a southern accent is so funny. We just can't stop laughing.

I ask Pops whether men really make love to men and, if so, how they do it?

"Don't know," he says. "Guess one bends over like a double barrel shot gun, while the other one fires him up from behind." We laugh so hard my side starts hurting.

"Remember, all men are not the same, so don't judge until you walk a mile in a gay person's shoes. Remember segregation. Just four short years ago White folks said you were just above a monkey, so don't judge gay folks just 'cause they are gay. Look at that piano player...what's his name? You know. Oh yea, Libericha. He's a genius," Pops says, still laughing.

"Pops, you know, the White boys up north are always talking about eating at the Y. But being gay and eating at the Y are two pairs of shoes I don't think I can ever walk in."

Pops makes lunch and gives me my treatment. He doesn't seem angry about Jade spending the night with me. This takes away some of the hurt of her leaving.

My treatments continue until the Christmas holidays when the gang comes home. They are no longer young boys and girls as I remember them in my mind, but they are now good looking young adults. Sun has changed the most, wearing his dashiki and sporting a big Afro. He looks out of place in Tryon, more like he belongs to a tribe in Africa. Almost every Black person he sees, he holds up his fist and gives the Black Power sign.

Head whispers in my ear, "We better hurry up and send Sun back up north 'fore these White folks down here kill his Black Power ass."

Fox is out of the service for Christmas and Jolene looks stunning with her west coast tan. Since Fox is getting some now, he still has a smile on his face. Head looks the same, as though he is still sixteen. We are a sight to behold around town spending time with each other talking about old times. We even go to the movie and sit downstairs with the White folks just because we can. However, spending time with and making love to Jade makes it my best Christmas ever. We plan to get married July the fourth next year, after she finishes college.

Spring comes like a gift from Heaven with all the blossoms on the trees, wild flowers everywhere. Maybe Spring just seems more vivid. Because of working with Pops, the pain in my leg is about gone. Other than a slight limp, I can walk almost like new.

I am at Pops' once a week, getting my treatment. I don't need it anymore, but Pops seems to want my company anyway. Most of the time we just talk, with no treatment. He has become like a father now and buddy at the same time.

"I am not supposed to say anything to you about this, so don't tell Jade I'm telling you. You promise not to tell," Pops says.

"Of course," I say.

"Jade wants the wedding to be in Asia, that way she can

see her homeland and show it off to all your friends. Look here, at my picture album. Let me show you some of my country, and of course me winning Marital Arts championships."

The album is very old like some of the old Bibles in people's houses. I enjoy the album and how handsome and well built Pops was when he was young. There is a picture of Jade's father and her mother holding her as a baby. Her mother was beautiful; I see where Jade gets her looks. I want to ask Pops about them, but remember he gets sad any time anything is said about them. Instead, he points to a picture in the album. It's the day he became the youngest ever to win this champion belt. His story is just getting good when the phone rings.

"Let me get this," Pops says. "I'll only be a minute." After hello and a few words he has this strange look on his face.

"There is something terribly wrong," he says.

Please don't let anything be wrong with Jade I think to myself. "Your Grandma says, hurry home! It's urgent," Pops says.

I run to the car, momentarily forgetting the pain in my leg as I speed home. Grandma is at the front door, holding a hankie, crying.

"Got some real bad news," she says.

"What is it?" I ask. "Are you alright?

"It's not me. It is your buddy Sun. He's been shot and is in real bad shape. His mother just called and wants you to pick her up and take her to the hospital up north. Use my car. It's full of gas and the keys are in it."

Without changing clothes, I jump in the car.

When I get to the house of Mrs. Mamie, Sun's mother, she is already outside waiting. We drive all night, arriving at the hospital early in the morning. Fox and Head are already there waiting for us, as we walk into the hospital.

A doctor comes up and tells us, "Sun has been shot several times and is in bad shape. We have him well medicated so he feels no pain. You all can go in, but can't stay very long. I think he's been holding on just to see you all, so go right in."

50
The Promise

We walk into Sun's room together. He has tubes everywhere; his eyes are closed. As we gather around his bed, his eyes open slightly. Seeing us, a smile tries to come on his face. He speaks in a very low voice.

"I know the White man's secret weapon. I told you he would have one." We look at each other, surprised Sun can speak.

"He's talking out of his head," Fox whispers in my ear.

Sun pauses, and says, "It's drugs and guns. Tell the Negroes to stay away from the drugs and guns. The White man is going to use them to destroy us. Make them cheap, so all the Negroes can get them and destroy themselves. I tell you, Whitey thinks way ahead of us on ways to keep us down. Don't let him do it. Okay. And tell our young sisters to keep their dresses down and legs closed."

"We will tell all the people, but you are Sun and you can show them the light when you get well, and tell them yourself!" Fox says.

"I want you all to make me a promise," Sun says.

We look at each other; Fox and I know better than to make a promise without first knowing what it is.

"We don't need nothing like that Adam's test on our back any more," Fox whispers to me.

Our best friend is shot and very weak, so we promise and then ask him to just tell us what it is.

"Why them Niggers shoot me?" Sun asks. "They even

shot Malcolm X. We were fighting for their rights and them dumb Niggers shot us. Why? Our fight is with the White man, not each other. Why didn't they shoot that mother Earl Butts or that Governor Farbust? I think it was one of them Crackers that said 'All Niggers want is loose shoes and tight pussy.' What a terrible thing to say about our people. That's the mother they shoulda shot."

We can see him laboring to breathe.

"Sun, stop talking and get some rest," Head says.

"Partner, you have talked enough. Get some rest and we will come back later after we go get lunch. Get some rest," I say.

But Sun keeps talking anyway.

"You all promise to bury me in the White cemetery in Tryon when I die, because even when I'm dead, I still want to screw with the White man. Every time one of them Crackers prays or puts flowers on the grave thinking it's for a White man, it will be for little old Black me," he says.

"Make 'em bury me at about seven o'clock as the sun sets in the sky. In the morning the sun will rise to a bright new day. Seeing the sunrise the Negroes can remember me and make it a bright new day for them. Do you promise to do it?"

We look at each other, then at our friend.

"Yes, we promise. But you ain't gonna die. This is a good hospital, so just rest and you will be fine."

"Why them Niggers shoot me? Remember, you promised," Sun says.

Then he just stops breathing. We all look at each other and can't believe our buddy Sun isn't breathing.

Mrs. Mamie starts screaming. The doctors and nurses

come in telling us to get out of the room as they start to work on him. After a while the doctor comes out to tell us what we already know. Sun is gone.

Later in the day we make arrangements to have his body shipped to Hendersonville, a town about ten miles from Tryon where all the Black bodies are sent. There is a funeral home in Tryon, but they don't bury Blacks.

As we head back to Tryon, Sun's mother cries off and on all the way. A sad road trip, made even sadder because I have no idea how we are going to bury Sun in the White cemetery.

I walk Mrs. Mamie to her front door and she says in a weeping voice, "It doesn't make any sense. My Son wants to be buried with White folks, since he hated them so much in life. But that's his death wish, so I know with God's help you boys will figure it out somehow."

"You are right, Mrs. Mamie. Somehow we have to do it. To make matters worse, my buddy Fox has to fly back to his army base and won't be back until the end of the week, just a day or so before the funeral. Head and I have to figure all this out ourselves."

"I am too hurt to be of any help, but you can use my name any way you want. Goodnight, young man, and thanks for taking me," Mrs. Mamie says.

I hear her start to cry as she closes the door.

The next day, I call Mark to tell him about Sun.

"Mark, my friend, I have some bad news for you."

"Me first," he says. "I took time off from college to figure out how to kill this man down the street without getting caught. I called Pops and he gave me some better advice on how to get the man back without killing him. This man raises and fights pit bulls. One got out, attacked and killed my dog, and best friend, Teton. I tried to break them up, and got bit myself. I wish I knew karate like you and Fox. I would have killed that damn dog and the owner too. Can you believe it? Even after months, I still cry and have nightmares about it. I have been in training for months to get this buster back."

"Shut up!" I yell in the phone. "I didn't call you up to hear you complain about some damn dog! Our friend Sun has been killed. Who cares about a dog at a time like this?"

There is a long silence, I start to wonder if Mark has fainted.

"Don't kid me about a thing like that," he says.

"I wish I was, but Sun is gone. Fox, Head, and I watched as he took his last breath. He still was talking bad about White folks till the end."

More silence, followed by sobbing.

"When is the funeral?"

"In a week or so."

"Let me know if you need help. I'll come down," Mark says, weeping as he hung up.

At just about dusk, I go to my spot on the hill, my special place to pray and meditate. I need to ask the Creator how to accomplish this impossible mission. This is the place where I let blood when Fox and I became blood brothers. The place where Jade let blood the first time we made love. Now I am bleeding, not real blood but in my heart and spirit. For my friend Sun.

51
Funeral

Stretching out my arms in anger I want to blame the White man, Black man, or anybody for Sun's death. The evening shadows behind me make my stretched out arms look like a cross.

I think of Jesus dying, hanging on a cross. Jesus calls on his Father Jehovah in his trying times, but who can I call on to heal my hurting?

Crows, blue jays, and other birds sing all at the same time. The wind howls like some coyote in the distance, as millions of lightning bugs are flashing in the trees all around, like flash lights blinking on and off. A warm, joyful, peaceful feeling comes over me like I have never felt before.

I can feel Sun's presence saying "All is well with me." In the shadow of my stretched out arms I can see the silhouette of the cross projecting the image of Jesus looking up, calling on his Father.

This is the answer to my prayer, although my real father isn't around, Pops, my father figure, is. He is the wise one for me to call on. My spiritual place, my spot, is giving me a moment of peace and the answer to burying Sun.

After a restless night, I pick up Head and go down to Pops. Over breakfast we tell him of Sun's wishes, and plead for his help.

"Your promise to your dying friend will be like a curse haunting you all through life if you don't do it," Pops says. He points to a vase full of flowers in the corner.

"See the yellow ones? They are artificial. Fools a lot of people into thinking they are real by deception. This is what you'll have to do. Just figure out how." He goes back to reading his bulletin.

Head looks at me with a blank expression. "Is that all the advice he has?"

"We are screwed. I'm going to call Mark to come down. Maybe he can help," I say.

"Hell no! Sun doesn't want White folks helping us. This is a Black thing,"

"Look, Head, you talking like Sun is still alive. Besides, Pops ain't Black, he's Asian. With him talking silly, we need all the help we can get. Unless you can provide a way to switch caskets, I'm gonna call Mark."

Head has a funny look on his face. He scratches his head and smiles.

"Hey man. What's Mark's number? I'll call him myself."

We are just about to walk out the door when Pops falls on the floor laughing, kicking his heels up in the air like he has lost his mind.

"The Sheriff just died, his funeral is six days from now," he says.

"Pops, I know you didn't like the Sheriff, but I don't see anything funny about him dying," Head says.

"I have the answer to your problem. It's perfect. Let's switch bodies. Bury Sun in the Sheriff's grave and the Sheriff in his. Never could stand that man. Found out not long ago he was the grand wizard in the Ku Klux Klan. He messed over lots of Black folks around here," Pops says.

"Just a few months ago he busted Shine's whiskey still. Took that old man to jail. Shine died a couple weeks later.

The Sheriff could have let him go. Shine never harmed anybody, so, I'm in this all the way with y'all because it will serve him right to bury his prejudiced ass for all eternity, with Colored folks."

"Great idea! But how are we going do it?" Head asks.

"Haven't figured it out yet. It will be quite a challenge, but we have six days to come up with a plan," Pops answers. We are feeling much better now that Pops is on our side.

Moving toward the gate, I can't believe my eyes. The Colored taxi pulls up and Fox and Jolene step out.

Fox comes over and hugs me, "I had some leave coming, and I been such a good soldier the company commander let me take 30 days leave. I had to come back home and be with my blood brother at a time like this."

Jolene comes over and also hugs me. "We all have to be together at a time like this," she says, just as Pops comes out.

Embracing Fox, Pops says, "Glad you all are back home. Now let's take a ride."

"I am wore out from all this driving. Left the army post early, went to pick up Jolene at the airport then drove here," Fox says, but gets in the car. No matter how tired, we never say no to Pops.

He drives us over to the big White church where the Sheriff will have his funeral. There is a funeral scheduled later in the day. We go in the church before the body arrives, looking around trying to figure out if we can somehow switch the Sheriff's and Sun's bodies right after they close his casket.

"It seems like too many people are around to do anything in here. Let's go and come back later to watch the funeral.

Maybe we can get an idea then," Pop's says.

We leave and drive to the funeral home where the Sheriff is laid out in this real nice casket. I have never been in a funeral home before. The smell of musty flowers, soft funeral music and looking at the dead Sheriff make me uneasy. For some reason, I want to smile, seeing the Sheriff dead.

I can hear Pops talking to the undertaker.

"Just want to pay my respect to the Sheriff. By the way, would you honor me by sending the same kind of casket to the Black funeral home in Hendersonville?" Pops asks. "My son just passed. It would be a great honor for me having him laid to rest in such a fine coffin."

"Consider it done. I'll make the arrangements right away," the undertaker says.

Fox says in a low voice, "I bet if he knew it is for Sun, instead of a son, he wouldn't be so agreeable."

"What a relief. Now all we have to do is switch the coffins somehow," Pops says.

We drive back to the White church, and stand outside to watch as they bring the casket out the back door of the church and put it in the hearse.

"I've got a great idea. Let's start a fire or have someone stop in front of the church and holler 'Black Power.' This should make the people around the hearse come up front to see what's happening. Then we can switch the caskets," Fox suggests.

"Great idea, Grandson. It might work, but let's get more than one idea. Hopefully we don't need to get any more people involved," Pops says.

The coffin is loaded into the hearse and driven about two miles to the graveside right across the street from the

184

Colored church. We notice after the worshiping part of the funeral, people get in their cars and go back to the church for fellowship and food, leaving two gravediggers to lower and cover the coffin.

"So far this is our best chance to switch," Pops says. "War and I are going up to Hendersonville so he can make all the burial plans, since Mrs. Mamie put him in charge.

"The Sheriff is being planted at one P.M. Saturday. Let's make Sun's funeral at seven the same day. I'm dropping you, Grandson, off at the bulletin office so you can write an article explaining why Sun wants to be buried at seven P.M.

"You know, as the sun sets and rises in the morning and all that, I'm sure all the nearby counties will pick up the story. It's going to be a big funeral."

It has been a long sad day, in and out of funeral homes. At last Pops drops me off.

"Make sure you call your White friend and tell him to get down here quickly," he says, as he leaves.

I go in the house and call Mark right away.

"Hey, Mark, Pops said you might help us. Can you come down?"

"You always tell me you and Fox never say no to Pops, neither can I. I'll be leaving early in the morning."

Sure enough the next evening Mark pulls up in a sporty looking van.

"My partner, War," he says, hugging me. "So glad to be back in Tryon, although not under these circumstances,"

"Get your stuff and come on in. Your room is ready. Grandma has food on the table."

"Wait a second. I have to feed my cat."

Mark reaches into a cooler, pulls out some raw liver and

sIt's cooling off, so ets it in a big pan. Then this huge tom-cat comes out and starts eating it.

"This is Teton, my cat. I just kept the same name as my dog that was killed."

I think to myself, "Mark seems a little strange. He is tak-ing this cat thing a little too far."

Mark wants to go see Rebecca; but instead we go down to Pops, where we discuss the problem of how to switch coffins.

We throw ideas around till late in the night. There are some good ones, and some crazy.

"We might go to jail for a long time if we get caught," Pops says. "Also you can't tell anyone about this. It must remain our secret for a long time. I have the plan. Leave it all up to me. I will give each of you instructions tomorrow. Goodnight, my children. Get some sleep."

The next morning is two days before the funeral. We go uptown to what used to be a White only café. I don't think any local Black people have eaten there yet. We walk in, and order country ham, grits and eggs. The White people are checking us out in a sly way. All of them, except this old gentleman who keeps staring at us like we're from outer space.

He doesn't seem to mean any harm, but with Rebecca being shoe-polish-black, Mark being a Jew, Fox and Jade Asian, Head with his long nappy head, Jolene being cream in your coffee, and with me being reddish brown, maybe he has never seen such a rainbow of color. Or maybe he just can't get over the end of segregation.

"Pops wants us to come down after breakfast," Fox says.

When we get there Pops shows us this old truck he borrowed from a neighbor. It has high sideboards and was once used to sell cut-up wood for twenty-five cents a bushel basket. In those days people had wood and coal burning stoves to cook and heat their houses. I remember that from when I was real little, but now everyone has heating oil.

Pops tells us to get in, girls in front and boys in back. Laughing and joking, it is fun till we pull up in front of Sun's mother's house. Laughter turns to sadness as we walk in the front door. It is made even sadder when I see Sun's closed casket in the living room.

"There's a lot to eat in the kitchen. Help yourself. Folks have been bringing food all day," Mrs. Mamie says. "When you finish, we'll pray and view the body."

Fox's voice quivers slightly, "We are not hungry right now, Mrs. Mamie," he says.

52
Sun Goes Down

Nonsense! Come on in this kitchen, hungry or not!
People just keep bringing food and more food.
Somebody has to eat some of this good fried chicken,
greens and sweet potato pie."

We sit down to eat, laugh and talk, momentarily forgetting about Sun.

"You're full now, so let's go view the body and say our
farewells to Sun," Pops says, as he puts a big Mason jar of
sake and some glasses on the table. We drink, telling stories
about Sun, singing some, crying some, anything to delay
viewing the body. This went on for a good while. I look over
at the Mason jar and it is empty. Then we hear the words we
are not looking forward to.

"Come on everybody," Mrs. Mamie says, as she goes
over to open the casket. A silence falls over the room.

Weeping, Jade grips my hand. We walk over and look
down at my friend. Having never been near a dead person
before, Sun looks as if he is just sleeping and at any moment
I expect him to jump up saying, "The White man still got his
foot up our behinds. Fooled you good this time, didn't I?"

Touching him, he is cold, like he is packed in invisible
ice. At that moment what I already knew, but just couldn't
bring myself to believe, I accept the fact he is not getting up.

For a moment I have this strange feeling of being born
again. My leg still hurts if I step wrong, so my movement is
slow. But, my friend will never see the flowers bloom in

spring, or the fall leaves turn golden brown in the mountain again, or know the warmth of a woman. It is like I have a second chance at life. My leg problems now seem so small.

The sadness and hurt of the last few days catch up with me. Tears flow uncontrollably like a river. Turning, I walk out on the porch.

Pops comes up behind me saying, "'Jesus wept' is the shortest verse in the Bible. So weep, my son. Some day you will weep for me or I for you, because the only person with you for your whole life is you. Be thankful and celebrate the time you had with your friend."

I turn and face Pops, the man I love and respect more than any, and I almost curse at him. This is one time his wisdom sounds trite.

It's not him I am really angry with; I'm just angry period, because my friend is dead. I have this sad feeling and a need to be alone, so I say goodnight and head down the path.

"Be here at eleven tomorrow with jeans and tee shirt," I hear Pops say. I have no idea what he plans to do, but I know, as usual, I must be here.

***

It's now the day of the funeral, by far the saddest day of my life. I sit in the swing, sawing back and forth. Grandma calls me for breakfast, but I tell her I'm not hungry. When my leg was broken I felt physical pain for a long time, but in the back of my mind I knew in time I could heal. This is pain in my heart and soul, and will never heal. Physical pain was never like this. Now I am weak and sad and just plain depressed.

At eleven sharp I walk up to Mrs. Mamie's house, in my tee shirt and jeans like Pops asked. I wonder if it is worth going through all the trouble to try and bury Sun in some White cemetery. The gang is already there, when I walk up.

Jade and Jolene have on black high heel shoes with very short tight black skirts. They look more like young hookers than someone going to a funeral. Pops puts them in the front seat of the old truck. I can't help but steal a quick glance at Jade's shapely thighs as she gets in the truck. Pops waves for us to come inside. We pick up Sun's coffin, carry it to the truck, and put it in the back.

Pops puts blankets over it, telling us to get in the back. There are rakes and brooms sticking up in the truck, making it look like we are gardeners.

Pops drives to the cemetery around back to the Colored section and parks. We can see the Sheriff's graveside with all the fresh dirt piled up. Just off to the side is the gravedigger's truck. Two men in bib overalls sit close by, drinking soda pop.

Pops gets out, studies the lay of the land for a long time, and then has a long talk with Jade and Jolene. He takes Mark off to the side and does the same with him. Now, it is our turn. When I put my hand up, Pops says, "Bring the truck around 'like a bat out of hell.' Like greased lightning, before quick can get ready."

"Okay, Pops, we get the idea," I say.

"Attention! Everyone gather around. I have explained how each of you must do your part to make this work. Does anybody have any questions? If there is anything not clear, now is the time to get it straight."

We all say no questions; we understand our parts.

"Good," Pops says, "Nothing to do now but pray and wait."

190

There is very little sign it will be a big funeral here today. That quickly changes as we see the hearse, a big black Cadillac followed by a long line of cars, slowly pulling into the graveyard.

A feeling of hopefulness comes over me when they take the Sheriff's coffin out of the hearse. It has a Confederate flag covering it, and several of the men in the crowd have Ku Klux Klan paraphernalia, waving little rebel flags, pictures of the Klan and such. The Sheriff's coffin is placed over the grave on a gurney.

The soldiers line up, and fire their rifles in the air. One plays *Taps* on his bugle, and the Sheriff's widow is given the flag off the coffin. It's very moving. People put flowers and things on the coffin as they file by, shaking the widow's hand, then walk toward their cars. This is an enlightening and a very impressive funeral with all of the regalia. I have never seen a funeral like this before. In my mind, there is no way we can pull this off.

Most people are gone now, as Pops walks down behind the gravedigger's truck. The widow makes her way to the car and now all are gone except the two gravediggers. One staggers slightly as he gets up and walks slowly toward the gravesite. I look closer at his bottle; it's corn whiskey, not soda pop he's been drinking.

They walk to the grave and prepare to lower the coffin in the ground when Jade and Jolene walk up in their short black dresses and high heel shoes looking sexy, waving.

"Hey mister, come here, please," they say.

One gravedigger, the one who was drinking the whiskey almost falls into the grave.

"Miss, can I help you?"

"Are we too late for Sun's funeral?" Jade asks.

"Sorry, Miss, but this is the Sheriff's funeral. That other black fellow's funeral is later on in the Colored church. Is there anything I can help you with?" he asks.

Pops sneaks up behind one of the men, putting him in a sleeper hold. He holds up his hand for us to bring the truck as he puts a sleeper hold on the other man. We hurry down with the truck. Within minutes, we put Sun's coffin on the gurney and the Sheriff's in back of the truck.

"Good thing the coffins are the same," Fox says, as we hastily head for Mrs. Mamie's house.

"Hey, Pops. Why did we leave Mark back at the gravesite?" Head asks.

"When the gravediggers wake up, they might become suspicious about the coffin. Mark is to ensure they bury it without any trouble."

"That White boy comes in handy after all," Head says.

We put the Sheriff's coffin in Mrs. Mamie's house and wait. About an hour later Mark comes in, jumping up and down, shaking everyone's hand.

"We did it! We just did the impossible," Mark says. "It was so funny, I wish y'all could have seen it when one of the gravediggers woke up and looked around, then at his whiskey bottle and said 'I got to stop drinking. I remember looking at these girls looking so hot they could raise the dead, then I just passed out.' It took me a while, but I got them calmed down. Sun is buried and covered up."

"Everyone quiet down. Let's not get too carried away. There is still a long ways to go," Pops says.

Our joy doesn't last long as we hear Mrs. Mamie crying in the next room.

The hearse pulls in the yard and this well-dressed man in black comes in.

"I am Mr. Jones, the funeral director. I'll take the body over to the church now. If everybody wants to come later, that's fine."

Mrs. Mamie has come in the room.

"Mr. Jones, we want to go with my son. It's a little early, but people will be coming in the church so we want to be there to greet them. Besides I want to spend the rest of the day near my son before he is put to rest."

53

White Man – Black Church

We load the coffin in the hearse and take it to the Black church. When we get there, lots of people are already outside, most with very sad looks. We roll the Sheriff's coffin toward the front of the church.

"I was raised in this church," I say to Fox, "and can feel it still vibrating from Mother Sunshine beating her tambourine while doing her little sanctified dance, and Mr. John Divine, Nina Simone's father, singing with his quartet. The only music they had was slapping their hands on the side of their pants leg, and the congregation rocking the church clapping and stomping with their feet. This is where Nina gets her soul from, this little church and old John D. Those were the good times and now we have the bad times."

"I don't belong to this church," Head says, "but the last time I did come it was to Candy's funeral when he got killed in Vietnam. He was one of the fellows and I liked him a lot, but Sun was like family. Candy's funeral was sad as hell, but nowhere near this sad."

"Before I went up north I used to come here every Sunday to Sunday school, and sometimes to church with Grandma, but this is my first funeral," I say.

"War, I bet this must be the first White man in this church in years, and he's not here by choice."

There are flowers everywhere.

Mrs. Mamie walks up and puts Sun's high school graduation picture on the coffin, then calls Mr. Jones and us to the corner of the church.

"I don't want an open casket with people staring at my child. All of these people came from out of town and most don't even know my son. I said my goodbyes last night and can't stand seeing him lying in the awful casket again. Mr. Jones, can you do me a big favor and make sure it's kept closed during the service?" She begins to cry.

"Mrs. Mamie, I assure you it will remain closed. Don't worry. Your wish will be carried out," Mr. Jones promises.

"Mrs. Mamie is good," Head whispers.

"She sure is. Let's hope it works," I answer.

By six o'clock, the church is packed. At seven, when the program starts, the crowd in the church has overflowed outside into the street.

Sun's militant group has sent several people down and the two biggest men walk up, standing on either side of the coffin, as if to protect it.

Fox and I are sitting in the first row with Mrs. Mamie, just like we are family. Fox leans over and whispers in my ear, "If someone came in here and tried to take this coffin, the two guards and the people would fight to their death. If they knew the Grand Wizard of the KKK was in it, we would have to fight to our death."

The preacher preaches about how this fine young man was cut down before his time. Listening to him you would have thought Sun was the next Malcolm. If he had lived, maybe he would have been.

As the program comes to a close, it is time for the people to file by the coffin and say goodbye to Sun. I can't believe all the people holding onto the coffin, crying, with others touching it, and some even kissing it. There are several

Black newspaper men here and even one from a White paper.

"With all these newsmen here," Head leans over and says, "we might end up in *Jet* magazine."

I am joined by Fox, Mark, Head, and the two big militant men as the pall bearers. This is the biggest Black funeral ever in Tryon. The sun is setting just like Sun wanted, as we drive the coffin around to the Black cemetery and bury it down on the steep hillside.

Head turns to me with a smile.

"I bet the Sheriff is turning over in his grave with all the Black folks buried around him," he says.

"Maybe so," I say, "but it doesn't matter which way he turns, he's still gonna see Black folks on either side."

The crowd is gone, with just Mark, Fox, Head and me left. Slowly we walk to the White part of the cemetery where Sun is buried. There are so many flowers covering the grave you can barely see it, but you can see the rebel flag someone stuck on the grave.

We stand around the grave, and talk to Sun just like he is alive.

"Even in death, my good friend," Fox says in a shaky voice, "you still have a sense of humor and you're still doing it to the White man. Can you believe what happened in just four short years? And you got to experience all of it.

"Martin was awarded the Nobel Peace Prize, and then assassinated. The Civil Rights Bill passed. They assassinated Malcolm X. Thurgood Marshall made it to the Supreme Court. There is the Vietnam War that took Candy's life, race riots, fires in the streets as Black folks tried to burn up L.A., Detroit and other cities, The Voting Rights Act, Black

Panther Party. Five Black players even started and won the college basketball championship. The greatest changed his name from Cassius Clay to Muhammad Ali. Your life was a short period of time, but so much happened, making it a full one. I read somewhere it's not how long you live, but how well and what you did my dear friend.

"This was really a season of struggle for the Black man. But what happened to my two best friends hurt me more. War's leg got all messed up and he can never play pro ball, but the most hurting thing is some Nigger killed you, my friend. You are gone, but will never be forgotten. Every time the sun rises I will see you."

"I remember the time we were arguing about Jews and Blacks," Mark says. "We talked about Adam and Eve and you said they had to be Colored, because two White people can't make a Black baby. Sun, there will never be another like you.

"We learned so much from each other about the struggles of our people, and in doing so we became good friends." Mark walks away crying.

"Growing up with you was so much fun," I say. "You kept us laughing and always in some devilment. You once said you would take a bullet for me. That's just how close we were. That's why I had to fulfill your last wish, even if it didn't make sense to me. Childhood was fun, but growing up is full of pain and disappointment. I will never forget you. Rest in peace, Old Buddy."

We all walk toward the street and home, with teary eyes and heavy hearts.

54
Cat

A sleepless night—I lose track of the number of cups of coffee I have. It's the first time in my life I watch night turn into morning.

Mark pulls up as I sit in the swing.

"I just came by for breakfast and to say goodbye before I hit the road," he says.

"I spent last night with Rebecca. She whipped that thing on me, cooked me some good old soul food, and, War, let me tell you, I am in love. We're getting married Christmas. Don't know how my parents will react, but this is my life. I have a favor to ask. Will you be my best man?"

"Sure thing! We could always use some more salt and pepper, but are you sure your Jewish ass wants to go Black?" I say, laughing.

"Stop joking about us. You can't talk with your half-White self. You got a whole lot of salt and paper in you. I'm pulling out in a little while, heading home, but before I leave, I have to give my cat a little workout."

With Sun's death, I haven't laughed much lately. But this is just too funny, especially with the serious look on Mark's face about his cat.

"You laugh, but Teton is not a regular cat. He is one in ten million," Mark says, with an angry frown.

"Come on. I'll show you. Can you take me to a hill without much traffic, *somewhere Teton can run behind the Van?*"

"Sure. In Tryon this isn't difficult. I'll take you to the

steep hill where Fox and I used to train. Fox nicknamed it the widow-maker after some hill he heard about."

When we got to the bottom of the hill Mark stops the van. "Come Teton," he says, and puts him out. He starts driving up the hill with the cat running behind just like a dog. At the top we stop, and get out of the van.

Mark lets the cat rest a while, gives him water and some cat treats. Then throws this small ball way down in the woods. Teton takes off like a scalded dog, leaping over small bushes, dodging trees until he gets to the ball. He jumps on it like a tiger, biting and shaking it like he wants to kill it. Mark whistles and in a flash the cat runs back up the hill jumping on Mark's leg right up on his shoulder.

"Whoa! What a show," I say. "How in the world did you teach a cat to do that?"

"The show isn't over yet. You talk bad about my cat. Watch this!" He ties a rope on a tree branch.

"Get to it, Teton!" he says.

The cat leaps up, gripping the rope, chewing and clawing on it, making little strings fall to the ground. A whistle and back on Mark's shoulder Teton comes.

I just buried one of my best friends, now it seems like this one is going crazy, taking the death of his dog and this cat thing way too far.

"Are you raising an attack cat in case someone breaks in your van and Teton can jump on them?" I ask.

"Don't be funny, but he might. I think I'll put on the back of my van BEWARE ATTACK CAT ABOARD," Mark says, laughing.

Back at the house, Mark feeds Teton a small raw T-bone steak. I watch as Teton chews and eats it like a dog.

"Mark, you are right! My hat's off to you! That is some cat!"

"It's been a fun, yet sad trip. Rebecca is so sweet, and spoils me with her southern cooking, but losing our buddy Sun took all the joy out of that…so sad," Mark says, pitching Teton in the back of the van. "But we must go now. I have a big favor to ask. In a few weeks, please come to the city. I need your help. Fox will still have some leave time left and he and Head have already said yes. Don't panic. I'll send you a ticket. I wouldn't ask if it weren't important."

"Hey, man! It will be a pleasure. Send that ticket. I need to get back there and take care of that fine Vickie anyhow." We shake hands, hug, and Mark is on his way.

The next few days are slow; a time of reflection on life. With my dagger and pistol, I decide to walk through the deep woods to Heaven. Maybe the river can help me deal with Sun's death. Walking through the woods totally alone for the first time is a little frightening. If my leg gives way, and there is no Fox or Sun to help, I could die. So I step carefully. I now have all the respect in the world for Shine; he lived alone in these woods making moonshine and survived for years.

There is so much activity; the little bugs scampering to and fro, the squirrels and the birds in the trees. The woods are full of life; yet, there is still a peaceful quietness about them as I walk slowly, taking in the sights and sounds. I stop at the springhouse the Cherokees built, and drink the pure cool spring water. I smile, thinking of the time we were naked here. I laugh as visions of Sun peeing in the river, while he swings at a big horsefly, flash in my head.

Arriving at Heaven, I sit by the old swimming hole in

deep thought, remembering all the great fun we had here. I watch the water as a big leaf slowly drifts by, flowing downstream out of sight. Sun's life was like that leaf—here briefly, then gone.

My life has been so full of excitement. Most of it I caused myself by working hard. Some by being lucky enough to meet Pops and follow his teaching. Knowing Pops is a blessing, but as in yin and yang, the opposite side is a curse. There is no guarantee life will be fair, or you will live a long one.

Sun pissed someone off and he's dead, and there is no pro ball for me. You can be here today, gone tomorrow. Even if you are here, there is always the pain of someone you love dying.

At that moment, sitting beside the stream, it's like I am the only person in a world with no cars, no people, and no sounds other than Heaven. Pops says listen to the river and it will speak to you. I look into the water for hours and nothing happens. I am just about to get up when it speaks. I don't know how, but the message comes through loud and clear. The message tells me I am an only child, but it's no good to be twenty years old and alone. At that moment I decide to go home and write Jade a letter asking her to marry me at Christmas. We can have a double wedding with Mark and Rebecca; invite my old high school buddies, along with Mark's Jewish friends. It will be good getting together. Now I have a purpose in life.

"Thank you, Heaven for getting me back in the saddle of life again."

I leave and go uptown to the post office to mail Jade's letter. There is no home delivery of mail in Tryon; people get their mail at a post office box. To my surprise, the box contains a letter from Mark with a round trip plane ticket.

The letter is short and sweet and just asks if I will come to the city next week. Fox and Head already said yes. "It's only for one Saturday night, but very important. I need your help."

I write back saying yes and am excited about going. This also will help get over Sun.

55
Tears

The next few days feel like a month. Finally it's the last day before I leave. I borrow my neighbor's bike and take a ride around the neighborhood to get some exercise and check it out. What I find brings tears to my eyes.

I ride up to the top of a small hill not far from my house. Off to the left side of the road is a small sign saying 'Good Shepherd Cemetery.' I park the bike and walk over to Mr. Brown standing by a fresh grave. He is a short dark-skinned man wearing bib overalls and big work boots, looking like he just finished plowing the back forty of his farm.

"Hi, Mr. Brown, how are you today?"

"Son, I'm lower than a well-digger's behind. I feel like I can't go on. I just buried my wife of forty years in the new cemetery. Since you went up North the town closed Tryon Cemetery. As a matter of fact, the Sheriff was the last person buried in the old one. The White folks are buried out in the county now and we're buried over here. Because of integration maybe they figured they would have to be buried side by side with Black folk and dead White folk just can't have that," he says, shaking his head.

"Funny thing though, by trying to get away from us, it's turned into a blessing for us. All the churches now can bury our folks over here and it makes it much easier to keep track of family members. Son, you know what, I never could quite understand was what made White folks think we want to be around them when they are alive, must less dead."

"Right you are, Mr. Brown, I wouldn't know any dead White folks anyway, but there are seven graves here and I know all the people. I went to church with some, and played with other kids. They were just like family. Your wife is in good company. So grieve a while, then enjoy life and be happy like she would want you to. I just buried my best friend. He was only twenty-two years old and it hurts. It's much easier to say start enjoying life than it is to do, but we both have to learn to carry on." I start back to my bike.

"Thanks, Son. It's been a pleasure talking with you. It's made me feel so much better. Thanks again. God bless and enjoy your bike ride."

I leave Mr. Brown still looking down at the grave, and ride down to the old baseball park. I feel sad as I look around at all the old tires and junk lying around. No more Saturday ball game and BBQ smoked over hickory wood so tender and good it makes BBQ up north taste like dry wood.

My heart is sad when I ride to the old store front where all the fellows used to meet after work to talk about ball games and chew the fat. It's closed. No more arguing about who's the best baseball player, Willie Mays or Hammering Hank Aaron. Even the cafes where people used to party on Saturday night are closed; folks from all around came to Tryon to dance, drink, and carry on. Tryon was the hot spot of the area. It seems like instead of making it better and opening things up, integration has done just the opposite and closed Tryon down for Black folks. So I wonder, other than going to their school, what's so great about integration?

I ride up to the old Tryon Cemetery to the Sheriff's grave site where Sun is buried. Mr. Brown was right. The Sheriff's headstone was special and about four feet tall, with the words hand carved into the stone.

The Sheriff is the last to lie in Tryon Cemetery.

May he find peace and keep the peace for all eternity.

After all the bad things I saw today with so many things closing this cheers me right up. To think Sun with his Black self is lying in the Sheriff's grave, with White folks making this grave the showcase. Keeping it clean and neat with fresh flowers for him is just downright funny. Now I understand why his last wish was to be buried in the White section. It looks like he is still doing it to the White man.

After my long bike ride, I have a good night's sleep and in the morning Grandma drops me off at the airport.

I am on the plane heading toward a completely different world—'The City.' Auntie picks me up at the airport. As we drive along the highway, I see many changes in the city just in the short time I've been away. But they are changes for the better, unlike Tryon where the changes are for the worst.

The next day, Mark pulls up in his van and out leap Fox and Head. We jump around, embracing each other like long lost brothers.

As the excitement of our meeting dies down, Mark says, "Let's get on the road. We have a couple of hours ahead of us."

I see Teton sleeping in the back of the van near a small cage.

"Listen, guys," Mark says. "This is very important. Just do what I say no matter what. If you have to pretend I am Pops, since y'all never say no to him—do so, You can ask questions later, when there is time to explain. Here is two thousand dollars apiece. Bet all this money on Teton, but first get all the odds you can. If you lose, you owe me nothing. If you win, give me my two thousand back and keep all you win. It's a sweet deal. But, you must bet on Teton, no matter what. Can I count on you all?"

Fox, Head, and I look at each other, shaking our heads because this is getting too weird.

"We are here to support you," Fox says. "Besides, the money part makes it exciting. So, lead us on, White Boss Man."

"Stop joking. This is dead serious. You must be at the top of your game, so rest your eyes until we get there," Mark says.

Some time later we pull up about a quarter mile away from this old barn way out in the middle of nowhere. We are close enough to see a few expensive cars, but mostly pickup trucks and vans are parked there.

"Game face on, boys." Mark hands Head a bow and arrow telling him to get out, sneak up and hide behind a clump of bushes near the barn.

"You are our cover in case we need it. Give Fox your money. He will bet it for you."

Head tries to say something, but Mark puts up his hand.

"Remember, no questions till later. Just be ready to shoot if necessary when we come out."

Mark puts Teton in this small cage, and then drives up to the barn. We get out and walk up. This old man wearing a straw hat and smoking the biggest cigar I've ever seen is sitting in a chair leaning back against the wall of the barn.

This must be a gambling joint or a ho house and he must be the lookout Mark mentioned.

Seeing us, he laughs.

"So, you boys are the cat boys. Welcome." He pats us

down and says, "No cameras or guns. You boys are clean. Go on in." I can still hear the old man laughing as we enter, We walk by some stalls, mostly empty, but a few with horses and a strong smell of manure. Way in the back is another room with just a little light coming from under the door.

Mark opens it. There are men sitting around in this circle of benches yelling, shaking their fists like they are at a prizefight. At the bottom is a pit where two dogs are fighting. One of the dog's legs is just barely hanging on, but he keeps fighting. He has the other dog by the neck. I watch the dog trying to free himself, but the other dog won't let go. Shortly, he lets go and the other dog is dead.

Some of the men yell, taking money from others who must have lost. The whole circle turns, pointing at us, laughing and waving money in the air. Fox asks Head why are all these people laughing at us and what the hell are we doing in here.

He doesn't answer, but points to a man sitting in his own chair like he is the Godfather.

He stands up, turns around to us, and says, "Hi, Markey. My name is Big Sal. I've invited all these gentlemen here to watch the fight. If you have your ten thousand I have my twenty. They begged me not to bet you, until I told them you wanted to bet them also. They all laughed and said we won't be too proud to take sure money. Again, are you sure you want to do this?"

"I didn't come all this way to punk out. The bets are down and covered," Mark says.

"I like your heart, young man, but since you insist on losing your money...bring out Rocky," Big Sal calls.

56
Big Gorilla of a Man

This big gorilla of a man comes out with a huge pit bull and walks to the center of the pit. The man has big hairy arms and kinda leans forward like a gorilla.

"Look at his face. It's ugly, just like his dog. Talk about people looking like their dog," Fox says.

The gorilla man takes out what seems like an old inner tube, and puts it in front of Rocky. He grips it, and the big man starts swinging Rocky around and around and the big pit holds on. The crowd claps and yells.

As Mark walks down to the pit with Teton, he tells us to bet all the money on Teton and to just make sure we get good odds.

"You don't think Mark is going to fight that pit with his cat, do you?" Fox asks.

"It sure looks like it. He ain't been right since that pit killed his dog. I just remembered. Rocky is the dog that killed him. Now I know why all those people were laughing at us bringing a cat in here to fight that monster."

"I bet Mark got some poison in his cat's fur, something to make the dog sick and keel over," I say.

Big Sal tells the crowd, "Pit folks have come from all over to see this fool's cat fight Rocky. Got the nerve to bet me big money and bet you too. So, let's wash the animals and get this circus over with."

"Wash. There goes the poison idea. I know we told Mark we would bet on Teton no matter what, but should we?" Fox asks.

"It's his money and we did promise. So let's at least get some good odds," I say.

"I have a thousand on the cat who will give me the best odds," Fox says as he holds up the money. It goes from four, to six, then ten. We wind up getting ten to one on all the money.

"Great odds for all the good it will do. A cat versus a pit bull is just plain dumb," Fox says.

Just then a man in an expensive three-pieced suit stands up and says to us, "I'll give you fifteen-to-one."

"Too late. We already have made our bet. I got three hundred. Might as well go broke," Fox says.

"I have three hundred also," I say. "We'll bet our six, if you put up fifteen to one."

"Done. If a cat beats Rocky, my money is well spent because I will have witnessed the impossible, a historical event that will be passed down like a Paul Bunyan tall tale," the man says, taking his money to the betting station where all the bets are kept.

Rocky and Teton are dry now. They place them at opposite ends of the pit, facing each other. Rocky is foaming at the mouth and Teton has the nerve to have his back hunched like he is stalking Rocky.

Big Sal says, "May the Lord forgive me for what's going to happen to this poor cat, but I must give the command to fight."

Rocky and Teton start toward each other. The pit goes for the cat; he is quick as his mighty jaws clamps down like steel vice just missing Teton. But Teton is quicker and dodges his teeth. Quick as a flash, Teton jumps on Rocky's back and with lightning strokes, rakes each of Rocky eyes with his razor-like claws.

The mighty pit is stunned. He instantly rolls over. Teton jumps off and, before you know it, goes around back and clamps down on one of Rocky's little brothers so hard it sounds like a crack, while he scratches his thing with both claws.

The pit with all his great fighting instinct, tries to reach back and grab Teton; but Teton moves the opposite way, making it look like a dog chasing his tail.

Teton lets go of Rocky's little brother and jumps on his back, rapidly clawing his eyes again.

Rocky lets out this strange sound, rears up like a great stallion and runs full speed into the side of the pit.

Teton jumps off, as Rocky bounces off the wall, staggering around like a drunken sailor. Teton immediately is on his other little brother biting down and chewing like it is a steak.

Rocky just passes out, lying down kicking and trembling like a dying bird.

The gorilla man runs out and starts to kick Teton but Mark whistles. The cat comes and runs up his leg right on to his shoulder.

A man goes down into the pit and gives Rocky a shot to ease his pain. His eyes and one of his balls are bleeding as they take him out on a small stretcher.

The gorilla man, as mad as hell, walks over to Mark saying, "Your cat messed up my dog! I should do the same to you."

"Your dog, Rocky, killed my dog right in front of me, so now you feel what I felt. If you want to fight about it, pick either one of my friends and put up some money."

The big man says, "Are you serious? I'll fight both of them at the same time for enough money."

"One is more than enough to kick your ass. I have all the money I won, well over thirty thousand good American dollars, that say so. Anybody want any part of it, at five-to-one, of course?" Mark says, looking in the stands.

An old man in the stands gets up saying, "Take your winnings and leave. Your cat did something we still don't believe, but the big man there, is an ex pro-wrestler and has been in the ring with some of the best. He will seriously hurt both of your friends at the same time."

"This is a fight, not a wrestling match. Anybody wants to bet?" Almost everyone in the stands heads for the betting window. Soon all the money is covered at five to one, and lots of people still want to bet on the big gorilla man.

Big Sal stands up and says, "Attention. I'll take all the remaining bets on Markey's friend." Back to the window people go.

I'm not sure who is more surprised at Big Sal, the gorilla man or me. The big man looks at Big Sal and asks, "How could you bet against me? You're going to lose your money. All the ass you've watched me kick you should know this one is personal and he's going to suffer lots of pain just like Rocky."

Still standing, Big Sal tells the crowd, "Before you bet, listen to what I have to say. I would have lost my house, Caddy, girlfriend, wife, maybe, even my life, betting against a cat beating Rocky. Anyone who can train a cat to beat a pit, my money is with them, even if they bet water won't make you wet, so all side bets I will cover."

"Nice speech, but this is man-to-man, so, let's bet,"

someone in the stands says, as they put money down on the wrestler.

I'm standing in the pit with Mark while Fox is at the betting table. The big gorilla man looks at me and says, "Come on. You're first. Get ready, because I am going to bust you up! Then wipe the floor up with your buddy."

Before we move, Big Sal says, "Hold up. Wait until all the bets get down before you fight."

Fox comes by my side, "War, let me take this. Your leg is not up to par and this joker is a load."

"No, Fox, he called me out. I got this."

Big Sal stands up. "Quiet, please. I have just been informed that all the bets are in. So that no one dies in this fight, or gets permanently injured. If either of you pats on the floor, or pats any part of the body, or if I blow this whistle, the fight is over. If you keep going you lose all your money. Understand?"

We both nod yes.

"Good. Now go get ready and in ten minutes come back ready to fight," he says, as he directs me to a bathroom.

57

Big Money

Fox and I go to the bathroom, a little room with just enough space to stretch and warm up. Throwing punches in slow motion with Fox, I am fine. However, any fast moves make my leg feel weak.

"Look, War, with your bad leg, let me take care of this big dude. You know you are not in any kind of condition to be fighting someone like him."

"Very true, old buddy, but this is something I must do, so please leave now so I can concentrate and center my mind and body. You know Pops taught us to find our opponent's weakness and overcome ours. This is one of the times I must overcome mine. I know you don't want me to lose all that money."

"Okay. Get yourself together, Blood Brother, and remember all the hills we ran, push-ups we did, and techniques Pops taught us. So, no slow moving gorilla will be any problem for you, but if you need me just holler."

Now I am alone and begin to think about how to fight the big gorilla of a man.

I must do something fast before my leg gives out. He is the most dangerous kind of fighter. He knows many different ways to hurt me. Besides being big, mean, and tough, he is very pissed off. If I didn't have this bad leg with my speed and power I could take him out easy, but now it will be more difficult, yet I must figure out a way to win.

The whistle blows for the fight to begin, all too soon. As

I walk down to the pit, it seems much smaller than before and the fighter much bigger.

I feel like a gladiator in Rome, fighting to the death in the Coliseum. I need something to motivate me, a reason to get in a fighting mood.

All the money at stake should be enough, but I need something personal to make me dislike this man. Then it comes to me.

Looking around the pit, I see the blood from all the dogs he made fight, suffer, and ultimately maimed and killed, all in the name of sports. This is breaking the law, and cruelty to animals.

The pit bulls have such a fighting spirit and love for him, till they suffer pain and even death to please him, yet he shows them no mercy. So, I must show him none.

Now I am motivated, looking across the pit at him. As he walks, his right leg has a slight limp. This is the weakness that Pops has taught us to look for in an opponent and where I will attack.

Big Sal says, "This is a street fight with no rules. Anything goes except the ones I told you about. Stop when I blow my whistle or someone pats the floor, or pats any part of the body, any questions?" We both shake our heads, no.

The crowd is on their feet, the noise deafening. I can hardly hear the whistle as Big Sal blows it and says, "Fight."

The big man comes at me like a bull charging a matador. Like a matador, I sidestep, kicking him hard with my good foot right on his bad knee. He dips slightly, but before he can recover, I kick him on the inside of his other knee.

He doesn't want to go down, but the next kick on his ankle makes it buckle. He goes down on one knee as I round-house, and kick him under his chin. Down he falls like a giant redwood tree to the floor, rolling around in agony.

I look at Big Sal. He doesn't blow the whistle, so I put the big man in a headlock and punch him in his face. Blood is running from his mouth and nose. "Pat the floor," I beg the gorilla man, but his pride won't let him. I look up at big Sal and he blows the whistle ending the fight.

The crowd is in shock. Somebody hollers, "The fight is fixed." Someone else yells, "Kicking is no way to fight, this ain't no football game."

Big Sal comes into the pit, holding up my hand as the winner. I look up and see Mark and Fox already collecting the money. The man in the three-piece suit walks up to the window also. He apparently bet on me.

The big gorilla man is moaning as they sit him up on a stool. I start up the steps, joining Mark and War on our way out in a hurry.

When Big Sal says, "Wait a second." My heart skips a beat and we are ready to run for the door.

When he says, "I have seen lots of unbelievable things in my lifetime, but never have I seen the likes of you boys. I have two men stationed outside waiting to take your money, but I am calling them off because I know they are out of their class." Big Sal, turns toward the crowd.

"Gentlemen please follow me outside just to see what would happen if my men tried to rob them. I hope you realize that although you lost lots of money, you have seen a show you will never forget or ever see again in your lifetime."

We all walk outside. The old man is still sitting in his

chair, leaning back against the barn, but not laughing any more. Off to the right is a big red CocaCola sign up on the barn.

Mark walks over and points up at it. An arrow comes out of the bushes, hitting right in the middle of the coke sign, making a slight vibrating noise, almost before Mark stops pointing.

"I am impressed. I just knew you had your escape covered. Here is my card. If you boys ever need anything, just call Big Sal." Turning to the crowd, he says, "I told you these boys are something special." The crowd starts clapping lightly at first, then it turns into loud applause.

We say goodbye. On our way to the van the man in the expensive three-piece suit, comes up to Mark, and talks with him for several minutes.

Waiting in the van, Head says, "Somebody tell Mark to come on. We need to get down the road while these men are still cool. After all, they done lost a ton of money."

Just then Mark gets in and started up the van.

"The crowd is getting restless. We better haul ass," he says, pulling away slowly. But soon as we get out of sight, it's pedal to the metal.

Driving back to the city, we keep looking back frequently to make sure we are not tailed. When we are satisfied no one is following, we stop and get some wine to celebrate. Then we drive to the middle of a big open field, where we can see all around, to divide the money.

58

Baby Makers

Fox takes it out of the bag and starts throwing it up in the air. "It's raining money. I am rich and didn't have to kick nobody's ass—but I ain't too proud to take my share. Now I can buy my baby boy a new pair of shoes. Thanks to his godfather's kicking ass. In case you didn't know it, War, you are the godfather."

"You got Jolene knocked up?" I ask.

"You better believe it, and my boy will be an Asian and Black mixed ass-kicking, name-taking, heartbreaker just like his dad and godfather. I'm going to name him Markey after the baddest Jew since Moses."

Mark takes out this bottle of kosher wine.

"Let's drink a toast to that. First, let me pour some on the ground for our missing partner, Sun, who will always be part of us."

Pouring our wine, he says, "I didn't tell you guys, but I got Rebecca pregnant. So we will have a Black Jew who will be a very rich lawyer some day. And Fox, you didn't know it but you are the godfather. You are now an Asian Jew."

"A toast to the baby-making Jew," Head says. "Let's drink to one hip cat. With one bad, ass-kicking cat that makes lots of money for us cats. And, of course, to our fallen warrior, Sun."

"My turn," says Mark. "A toast to three friends who without asking why, came to help me. And, War, thanks especially for being my buddy when you could have chosen any-body. One more thing—while the Godfather was telling y'all how great you are, I was talking to the man in the three-piece suit. I'm going to work for his company next week. Can you believe it?"

"What you gonna do?" I ask.

"I have been looking at this stock thinking it's going to take off, and the man in the three-piece just confirmed it. If you let me invest y'all's money, it should double in a year or so and in five make you rich. All in favor of me investing it, raise your hand."

"Jew boy, we are all in. You done made a believer out of us. Go make us rich, but first let's all give Mrs. Mamie a few thousand dollars apiece as part of Sun's share," Head says.

"Great idea, she can buy herself something nice to help ease the pain of Sun's death," Fox says. "And, War, when you and my sister have a baby, it will be part Black, Indian, White, and Asian. I can't wait to see what my nephew or niece looks like…or what they will say when asked what race they are," Fox says, laughing while he throws money up in the air.

"Enough of this sentimental stuff. Let's take a couple of hundred for pocket money and give the rest to our stockbro-ker, drink some wine and tour our city. With all this baby-making going on, y'all definitely don't need to look for no women. So, let's tour and do the White folks culture thing. Please pass the wine bottle," I say, laughing.

"This wine has me feeling like I'm a king," Fox says. "I have two pockets full of money. A sexy woman is waiting to turn me on when I get home. Life is good. But before we go further, we have some unfinished business with our Mr.

Jewish Genius buddy here. I'm not going to spend the next hundred years of my life wondering how Mr. Genius trained a cat to whip a pit bull. I spent enough time as a little boy wondering how Santa could fly round the world in one night, and don't need to go crazy trying to figure this out. So start talking, Mr. Genius."

"Come on, fellows," Mark says. "You know a magician never reveals his trick. Besides it's good to keep a little mystery in your life."

"Yo, Markey," I say. "Before you start this van, if you don't want your behind kicked, you best talk. Fox is right. Like fools we just went into the pits of hell with you, and came out like sissies in Boys Town. So, if you don't want your good luck turning bad, start talking."

"Okay. Since you are my boys. But, you know if you lay one finger on me, my Attack Cat has two paws full of razors and will cut you every way but loose. Alright, the truth. I know you all think I'm a genius…I am, but I didn't teach Teton to scratch a dog's eyes out. I don't think anybody can teach a cat that."

After a pregnant silence, Fox says, "Come on, man. No BS. If you're gonna tell us some jive story about how you sent away for him in some animal catalog, it ain't gonna fly. So close up this mystery in our lives."

"Okay," says Mark. "To make a long story short, Teton was Shine's pet. He was raised wild in the woods. He grew up eating raw fish, Shine's table scraps and drinking water from a stream. This sharpenened his animal instincts. He probably hunted for lots of his own food. Anyway, Shine brought him to town one day and a dog attacked him. His instincts kicked in and he jumped on the dog's back and attacked its eyes." Mark looked at us for a moment, then continued.

"When the pitbull killed my dog I was going to shoot him and his master. I couldn't give a damn about going to jail. Luckily I called Pops first. Pops told me about this cat. He said there were several dogs around town that everyone thought 'coons had blinded. Until one day his neighbor, Mr. Johnson, was walking his real mean German shepherd in a field. The dog spotted Teton and attacked. Mr. Johnson couldn't believe how fast the cat was on his dog, clawing his eyes. By the time Mr. Johnson got to them the cat took off fast leaving his shepherd rolling around with blood coming from its eyes." Mark took a breath.

"Pops told me to come to Tryon and cool off before I did something stupid. We could go down to Heaven, do a little fishing and meet Shine and his cat. So I came to Tryon. I didn't see any of you, even Rebecca, because my head was all screwed up. Pops took me down in the woods to meet Shine. I was so impressed. Never in my life have I met a man like him, a true man of the woods. We even camped overnight with him. He showed us rabbit traps, and how he got honey from the bees. What an experience that was, spending time with him. Then when he felt at ease with me he gave me Teton. 'I'm glad to give him to you,' he said. 'Now people know it's Teton not 'coons. They said they gonna shoot him on sight.' Shine looked me in the eye. 'It wasn't Teton's fault,' he said. 'They wanted to kill him. He was just protecting himself. If someone kills my cat, my best friend, I'd get in trouble. I have a temper and there's no knowing what I might do. So take him and give him a nice home.'

"I guess I didn't make a long story short," Mark says, "but now you know all I did was get him in tip-top shape, and taught him to be okay around people."

"Wow! What a story," Fox says. "Now when I tell my son of our great adventures at least the story of a cat beating a pit bull will make more sense than Santa flying around the world in one night.

"Now, crank up this van and as Shirley and Lee say 'Let the good times roll.' Take me to the best steak house in town. I have two pockets full of money and I'm king for a day."

Me and Mark give Head and Fox a grand tour of our city and then take them to the airport. We watch as their plane climbs higher and higher in the sky till it is out of sight—knowing they might be out of our sight but, never out of our hearts and mind.

Mark drops me off; I pick up my car and head for Vickie's house. I have lots of money and no Adam test to stop me from making love to this fine young lady. This should be the happiest time of my life, but I feel an emptiness I never felt before.

There is no river Heaven, or my favorite spot on the hill to go to, or even Pops to talk with and find out why I feel this way.

The first eighteen years of my life have been full of excitement, and adventure, learning, and experiencing so many new and wonderful things. My first time getting some, first airplane ride, even saw the end to segregation, but what do I do now?

I see a small park with people walking, so I pull over and get out of my car. I walk over to a bench, sit and watch people walking by. Most are overweight, as if walking a few laps will repair all the damage done to their bodies over time. Some are even smoking, others built real funny. As I watch I realize even with my bad leg how blessed I am. I think of my buddy John and all the girls he is making out with, yet he doesn't seem happy. While Fox only has one woman and can't stop grinning.

I'm starting a new chapter in life where it's just me; all my buddies I grew up with are out doing their thing. I think of Pops and the yin and yang he talks about. 'Night-day, life-death, God-Devil'. This is my yin and yang, Vickie or Jade. Vickie would be fun for a short time, much like following the Devil, but Jade is fun for a lifetime. She not only is my lover, but my friend. I realize my love for her is stronger than any Adam test, but that was forced on me. Yet I choose to be true to Jade.

As I sit on the bench people watching, I figure out my emptiness is caused by going to make love to Vickie and not being true to Jade. I stand up and my emptiness is replaced with a joy that makes me smile just thinking of seeing Jade and feeling her next to me.

I will spend a few days in the city with Aunt and Uncle, and say hey to a few friends. I'll go to see how the little boy whose life I saved has grown and let his mother fix me a nice dinner. After that I'll get in my car and head home to my beloved Jade and all the people that make Tryon so special.

59
1970: A New Decade

Driving along the highway looking at the changing scenery, I have lots of time to think. I realize for the first time in my life I'm totally alone. Even when I first went to the big city there was Aunt and Uncle, but now, just me. Already there is a slight chill in the air at night; old man winter is not far away. I feel the need to be alone and get to know myself, so I keep driving till I get to the Sunshine state.

Winter comes and the best thing about the Sunshine state is there is not much winter. The warm weather and just relaxing on the beaches, eating lots of different foods, and watching ladies with very little clothing on, renews my soul.

New Year's Eve is a blast. I watch as people celebrate the coming of a new decade, like everything will change and the 'seventies will be Utopia. But the day after New Year's nothing has changed—young men still dying in Vietnam, crime everywhere, and I have had enough of the Sunshine state. So I head for home.

I drive leisurely back South. Upon arriving in Tryon, everything looks so small. As a boy I walked everywhere, and Tryon was like a giant playground. Now the streets, houses, even the town seem much smaller than I remember. Pulling up to our house, Grandma comes out.

"Boy! Look at you. You've grown into a big strong good looking young man! See? I told you all the greens, okra, and tomatoes out of the garden you used to complain about were good for you. I'm glad you're big and strong 'cause I got lots of work for you to do around here."

"Grandma! You could say 'Hey, how you been?' before you start talking about doing some work."

"Hush boy. Come over here and give me a big hug, so we can go inside and eat. I got supper on the stove. I even made your favorite candied sweet potatoes. Oh yeah, before I forget, some man named Big Sal has been calling here for you."

"Big Sal? What did he want?"

"Didn't say, but he did leave a number for you to call. He said it is important. The number is in your room, on the dresser."

I call the number but there is no answer. I try again in a few days, but still there is no answer. Weeks go by without a call from Big Sal. There is so much to do I forget about Big Sal.

I spend time working around the house, raking leaves, painting the house, and other odd jobs Grandma comes up with.

My leg feels almost like new, except sometimes when it rains, or I step the wrong way, I am reminded it's still not one hundred percent. I go for hikes in the woods, sometimes taking Doby with me. I fish and swim in Heaven, drink water out of the spring house the Cherokees built. I never dreamed that just wandering in the woods alone, or with Doby could bring so much peace and contentment; it's like being in tune with Nature.

One day while I'm sitting on the bank of the River Heaven, a herd of deer come and drink. After drinking they wade down the river until it gets deep. Then they swim across to the other side. Even deer enjoy Heaven. The woods are never boring, because everything is constantly changing. The bare trees look like giant sticks growing out of the earth. It's hard to believe in a few months they too will change and be full of colors.

The 'sixties had come to an end, a violent decade of riots, fires, assassinations of Martin Luther King Jr., John and Bobby Kennedy, Malcolm X and the end of official segregation. It was one hell of a decade to grow up in. Although it was only six years ago, in 1964 when the south was still segregated, and Blacks had no rights, it seems like a long time ago. Even with all the turmoil in the 'sixties, they still manage to put the first man on the moon.

It's 1970, a new and exciting time to live in and see what new things are in store for me. I'm twenty years old, a strange age, no longer a teenager, and yet not completely an adult. Old enough to go to Vietnam and die, but not old enough to go to clubs, or buy a beer. I'm sitting in the swing on the front porch drinking a glass of cold lemonade and eating a piece of lemon meringue pie when, to my surprise, Pops and Fox walk up. I jump up and run down to greet them.

"My two grandsons are now grown men." Pops says. "All the hell I put you through, with long workouts, making you run, throw punches till your arms felt like they would fall off, and exercise sometimes for hours. My time spent teaching y'all martial arts and how to be gentlemen has paid off. You two make me proud. I want to run something by you two. I think it's a golden opportunity for both of you."

"Pops, it's nothing like that damn Adam test you made us go through, where we couldn't get any until we were eighteen, I hope?" Fox asks, laughing like he's just heard one of Richard Pryor's jokes.

"This is much more serious. For the last few months, I've been to Washington, D.C., several times. It was one of the highlights of my life to see all that history: the White House, Lincoln Monument, the place where King gave his 'I Have a Dream' speech. I got to see it all in real life. They paid my way there just to ask me tons of questions about you two. Speaking of history, it's us they were interested in. They went over our history front and backwards, checking us closer than a preacher can clean a chicken bone. We have top secret clearance. To get to the point, you two are not going to Vietnam. Fox, you have finished your service time, and War because of your leg you were not drafted. They want to know will you join the Secret Service. You will only answer to me, or the man you met at the dog fight they called Big Sal."

"Pops, this is a joke, right? And by 'they', you mean the Government?" Fox asks.

"My sons, I'm not talking about just the Government, but the very top of it. So high up y'all will be like James Bond, the movie star—007. Your only contact will be with me or Big Sal. That is, if your answer is yes and you can pass three tests."

"Hey, Pops, I like this. Give me my gun. There are several folks in Hollywood I am dying to shoot," Fox says in a joking manner, "but why in the world'd they pick us, and how did they find out we're some bad sons of guns? Blacks and Asians just got off the plantation a few years ago in '64. What makes you think they're gonna let us join the Secret Service?"

"Grandsons, this is no joke. You two have some of the best martial arts training in the world. You are young, good looking and strong. The only thing I am allowed to tell you is Big Sal talked to several of the boys you beat up in the Karate Championship, and he saw War beat the big gorilla man. He is the one who recommended you. With affirmative action raising hell about Blacks and Asians not being in Government jobs, the Secret Service wants you two badly. Have you read the book called *The Spook Who Sat by the Door?* This should be right up your alley, maybe all they want you to do is sit by the door and be seen, to get the affirmative action requirement off their backs. So what? The pay is huge. Also in twenty years you can retire and still be a young man. Fox, your service time will count towards your retirement.

"I must warn you, if you say yes, as I said, there are three tests you must pass to be accepted in the program. This is serious business. If you need a little time to think it over, that's fine."

"It's okay with me." I say. "I was just about to go up north and take the post office test, drive a Greyhound bus or find me some city job. I am too young to be around here having Grandma work me like a hired hand. If this is real, it sounds exciting. If the pay is like you say, my answer is definitely, yes."

"I'm in also." Fox says. "Someone has to look out for my blood brother, and besides, I need a rest from Jolene. God knows I love that woman, but we're about to love each other to death. Since I got out of the service my job working in the movie business is boring and just plain dull. Even worse is putting up with all those queer people. I need some real life excitement."

"Okay. Big Sal will call you in the morning to tell you about the test. He is our boss, but you two will be working closely with me. One more thing is, if you sign up for this, you must agree to do whatever Big Sal or I tell you to do, without asking any questions. Do you have any questions, now?"

"No, Pops, we don't have any," Fox says. "Besides, we trust you, and this sounds like fun. So let's get the show on the road. And if this is for real, when does the pay start?"

"Raise your right hand and put your other hand on this Bible. I will swear you in, if there are no more questions. This in no way means you are in the Secret Service. You are only swearing not to tell or talk to anyone about this. I know if you give me your word you wouldn't tell anyway. But Big Sal wants you sworn in, read over these papers carefully and sign. It's something about making it legal, to protect the Government. Just in case one of you gets hurt."

Pops swears us in and says, "Now there are two ways we can do this. Number one is you will be a regular Secret Service person. This is a nice duty, where you work with the law enforcement agencies to help in their investigations. Or number two is like the Green Beret, a very special unit. Only about three out of a hundred get the chance to try out for this duty, and most of them don't make it. Which do you want?"

"Come on, Pops! You know we want number two. Besides, after all the training and hard work you put us through, this test will be a piece of cake," I say.

"Since you boys don't want a few hours to think of what you're getting yourselves into, and you want to join the special unit, remember there are three extremely difficult tests you must pass before you can become officially secret agents. If you pass the first one you will be given a charge card. With it, you can pay for your food, hotels and any small stuff you need. This will be good until you pass or fail test number two," Pops says.

"Remember just like a soldier in the war in Vietnam," he went on, "if you choose number two, you might be asked to kill someone for your country. In your mind, if you don't think you can kill someone if called upon, if any doubts, please take number one. So before the first of the three tests starts, once again are you sure you want number two?"

"Come on, Pops, we already said we want to be the next James Bonds. Neither one of us wants to sit around some dull office. Bring on test number one so we can get our credit card. Are you sure they're going to give minorities like us, that kind of credit card?" Fox says.

"Enough talking, y'all choose option number two, so let the test begin. See those six men coming this way? Since you want number two they are coming to beat you up. I told them to send eight men to make it a fair fight. They laughed at me and said six is overkill. So, get ready to take them out. This is test number one. I gave them the signal to hurt you, so, you had better get your game face on, grandsons, or I will see you in the hospital."

"Pops, what have you got us into? You telling me this is for real, not Hollywood stuff?" I ask.

"You two make a deadly team. I know it and so do the folks from the Secret Service. With your color, great bodies, and martial arts training you're both unique. War, you are at home with the Blacks, and with your light skin you can fit in almost anywhere. Fox, you have the Asian community

229

covered. That's why they want you two. The unit has sent their six best men to kick your butts, since I told them eight would be better to make it a fair fight. Good luck! You two are in for a serious fight," he says, as he walks away.

"Gee, thanks, Pops, for doing us such a great favor. Sure you won't stay and help?" I ask.

60
Test Number One

The six men split up into two groups. As one of the three comes after me, he lets out a karate yell and kicks at my ribs. I block it with my arm and dive into his other leg, taking him to the ground. I punch him hard with my elbow in his solar plexus, the sweet spot, or 'S spot' as Fox and I call it. He struggles for breath as I jump to my feet. The tallest of the three throws a punch at my face. I drop to a squat and punch him in his two little brothers—the 'B spot'. As I stand, I catch him under his chin with a punch. The third man attacks throwing fast punches. I block and weave, and round-house kick him upside his head and he is out cold.

Turning to look at Fox, I see two men out cold on the ground and the third one is real good. He and Fox are having a close battle until Fox catches him with a side kick on his chin—the 'C spot'. The man falls and does not move.

Walking over to Fox, I ask "Hey, partner! What took you so long? I started to come over and give you a hand."

"Screw you! They know how good I am, so they sent the tough ones after me," he says.

Pops comes over, saying, "Wow! What a show! I sho' taught you boys well. Y'all kicked some big time butt and aced test number one. Let's go."

Several medics comes across to work on the six men.

"You boys did well. I see most of my teaching got through to you. The medics were supposed to be working on you. I bet they are surprised to be working on the Unit's so-called best. You won't see me for some time. They want me out of the picture for a while—just want to deal with you. Be brave and good luck on your other two tests." Pops hands us each a credit card with our pictures on it. He turns and walks away.

"After kicking butt, I'm hungry! This is my first charge card. Let's hit the restaurant, get a big steak dinner and see if this puppy is real," I say.

It is.

About eight the next morning the phone rings. Grandma answers.

"Come and get the phone," she says.

It's Big Sal. "Welcome to the program. In case you boys are wondering about me and those fighting dogs, I infiltrated one of the biggest dog fighting rings on the east coast, in order to bust a big time drug dealer. He was selling drugs to kids, even in grade school. I sent his ass upstream without a paddle. If you don't wash out of the program, this is the kind of undercover work you will be doing. Now you two be at the front gate at Fort Bragg tomorrow morning at seven." Then the phone went dead.

I hang up the phone and go to get a cup of coffee. I sit and think about what I've just heard. The phone rings again.

"Hey, partner! What time do you want to head for Bragg? I just got off the phone with Big Sal. He told me he called you."

"What about noon? I'll drive. It takes about two hours to get to Bragg. We can stop somewhere to eat and find a hotel before dark, or we can leave about four tomorrow morning and drive straight through."

"Come on, partner! We have charge cards for hotels.

We're in the big time now. You got to stop thinking like we still under some stinkin' Jim Crow law. We need to go into a nice hotel, eat a nice supper and get some rest on a clean nice bed, 'cause who knows what test number two will be like?"

"I'm taking my car just in case there is some funny stuff and we have to make a quick get away."

"It sounds good to me. I'll be ready! See you at high noon," Fox says.

***

We pull into Fayetteville just on the outskirts of Fort Bragg about dusk, park and go into the finest hotel around. We walk up to an old White man behind the desk with thick glasses and a long White beard, looking like somebody left over from the 'sixties.

Fox says, "Sir, give us the best room you have in the house with double beds."

"Our rooms are kind of pricey," he says. "Sure you boys don't want to go down the road a piece? The rooms are more reasonable down there."

Fox starts to say something, but I push him away and say, "Sir we just left from down there and we saw some Colored boys going in the rooms with White girls. Lord knows what they gonna do to them White girls. They will be screaming and hollering all night, so we came up to sleep with you White folks where it's nice and quiet. We can't stand being near them rowdy Colored folks."

The old man is speechless, just standing there with his mouth open and a blank look on his face.

Fox hands him the charge card, and when it comes back approved, the old man manages to say, "Room 246. That's

233

the best room we have."

On our way to the room Fox says, "War, you got to stop messing with White folks. This is a new day; so, come off that doing it to the White man thing! I bet that poor man can't sleep tonight thinking about White girls with Black Boys."

"You're right, but that man was saying in so many words we don't want Black or Asian folks in our hotel, so I had to mess with him a little bit."

61
Test Number Two

The next morning at seven sharp we pull up to the gate at Fort Bragg. An older tough looking sergeant with stripes up and down his sleeves and a Ranger patch on the shoulder of his uniform comes over.

"Get out of the car and follow me," he says.

We walk to a field.

"Halt! I understand your nicknames are War and Fox," he says. "The troops called me Bloody Burns. That's my nickname, but you call me Sergeant. I am fifty-five years old, 185 lbs of rompin' stompin' Airborne. Wine and women are no good! Airborne is so good! In two weeks I retire. This gives me two weeks to teach you what it took me thirty years to learn. So there is no time to waste. You are in Fort Bragg, the home of the 82nd Airborne, the greatest fighting force on earth, and I don't like anyone that ain't Airborne! Meaning you two! I understand you are martial arts experts. I've been in the troopers thirty years and kicked many punks' asses like you. Does one of you want to try me? I love to kick ass 'fore breakfast."

"Sergeant, we would not lower ourselves to attempt to try you. You are the master, we're the students," Fox says.

"Yes Sarge. How will we learn if you don't teach?" I ask.

"You boys are getting off on the right foot with me. They told me you were wise beyond your years, but that sweet talk ain't gonna stop me from bringing smoke on your ass. Go to the building over there on your right and get your army clothes, so you will at least look like a soldier. After that, go to the mess hall and chow down. Meet me back here at nine."

After chow, we spent the next several hours doing PLF—parachute landing falls—which is how you land after jumping out of an airplane. We are put in a mocked-up parachute with a suspended harness hanging in mid-air, where you must be real careful not to get your little brothers caught in the harness. Finally we jump from a 30 foot tower several times in a harness shaped like one on a parachute, connected to a long line until we learned the correct way to jump out of a plane.

Then the unthinkable, Sergeant Burns says, "You boys are fast learning, so, if you don't have any questions, let's take a ride down to the airfield, get in a plane and go airborne."

"Sarge, does that mean what I think it means?" Fox asks, as two troopers come over and put parachutes on our backs.

When we get to the field the Sarge says, "Follow me, boys," as he enters the plane. "Let's see where your heart is and if you have what it takes to be Airborne."

The plane takes off and in no time it seems like the Sergeant says, "The drop zone is coming up. Hook up your chutes to the static line and stand in the door." With the noise in the plane I can barely hear Fox say, "For the first time in my life I am scared to death."

I am in front of Fox and tell the Sergeant, "I don't think I want to go."

When he kicks me out the door, I tuck my body like I was taught in training. I count, "One thousand one, one thousand two, one thousand three, one thousand four."

Then I look up and see this beautiful white open chute, and I say, "Thank you Lord." I look down at the ground coming up like it's in slow motion, with an eagle eye view of the whole surrounding area. The air is still and quiet as a graveyard at midnight; I drift down like a bird and come to a perfect landing. Fox lands not far from me. We both are so happy to be on the ground.

"Wow! That was a blast!" Fox says. "I was so scared before we jumped. My knees were shaking. This is a groove, I hope we have to jump some more."

The Sarge comes over when the plane lands.

"You boys did well," he says. "Here are your backpacks. Each has a half tent in it and a bed roll with everything you need. Go get some chow. After chow, Private Jones will show you how to set up your tent, how to use everything, and also where you will camp for the night."

"Sarge, you mean after all the hard work we did today, we have to sleep in a tent?" I ask.

"No, you don't have to! You can just sleep on the ground if you like. I suggest you sleep somewhere 'cause I'm bringing smoke on your behinds about five in the morning."

The next day we shoot every kind of gun the army has: pistols, rifles, big guns, little guns, and then we watch films on guns. The third day we are back in the plane and jumping into the Navy Seals' training site with Sarge right beside us. We learn to scuba dive, night vision training, and all kinds of things about maps. In the two weeks, we get about four hours of sleep at night. The Navy Seals have what they call 'hell week.' We have two weeks of hell.

At last it is our final day. After breakfast Sergeant Burns calls us to his office.

"You boys are all they said you were. We put you through some of the most intense training anyone has ever been through and you didn't complain once. You would make good paratroopers, but Sam has something else in mind for you. Now before I give you test number three, are there any questions?"

"Yes, Sarge. You never told us why they call you Bloody Burns," I ask.

"In jump school when a recruit comes in with fuzz on his face, I rub my hand across his face and if I feel it, I make him go dry shave in cold water with a dull razor and most of the time they bleed. Plus, I bring blood on their ass. Funny how after the first recruit shaves, I don't seem to have any more coming to jump school with fuzz on their faces. Are there any more questions?"

"No, Sarge, we are dead tired. So give us test number three so we can get some sleep, unless you want to tell us why y'all putting us through all this hard ass training."

"When they ran your history," he says, "the one thing they admired about you more than any other is, Fox you don't cheat on your wife nor, War, do you cheat on your girl friend. This more than anything shows your character and what kind of persons you are. This is the one thing I'm sad to say. They want to know if you could cheat for your country. Killing someone for your country might be easier than cheating. By now maybe you figured out test number three."

62
Test Number Three

It's that you both must cheat on your women. This might be fun. The only catch is it must be in Washington D.C., with two different women within two weeks," he says.

"Open this package when you get near D.C. Other than that you can go home, take a two week rest period. One month from today you both must have seduced two ladies you don't know at the present time in D.C. No hookers! The good news is you can wine and dine using your charge cards. Your limit is very high. So enjoy Chocolate City. In case you don't know it, that's the nickname of D.C. With its seven women to one man, and most of them a delicious chocolate color, even you two might get lucky. It's been nice knowing you." He gives a crooked smile.

"I don't know who gave the orders, or why y'all were put through all this training, and don't give a rat's ass. I'm headed to Florida to start my retirement. So have fun in D.C. trying to get some.

"Before you leave make sure all the trucks you see pulling out have cleared the company. Those troopers are headed for Vietnam. If I weren't retiring, I would be right there with them. Goodbye, you two. I'm going to the mess hall for my last meal before heading for the Sunshine state, for some serious fishing, and drinking."

There's sadness about the Sergeant as he walks away, still strong and capable, at fifty-five. "He still can out-soldier most troops. What a man!" Fox says.

"Fox, you drive. My leg is throbbing after all this Army stuff. Plus, I can barely keep my eyes open," I say, as I get into the passenger seat.

"Stop using that leg as an excuse, because I'm just as tired as you, but I'll take the first shift," Fox says.

"Tell me are we going to cheat on our old ladies? Jolene is all the woman I need or want. The idea of being with other women, I'm not so sure about that. When she puts on her purple negligée and that fancy perfume…'My! My! My!' take a look at my arm, I get chill bumps just thinking about her. What more could a poor boy from Carolina want? To mess my good thing up with another woman? I don't know about that."

"That's enough about your sex life, unless you want me to tell you about your sister. She walks around with people saying, 'she's so nice and sweet,' but they don't know she is a freak in the bed, and I love her and don't need no woman on the side! So are we going to cheat or not? Damn if I know! Go on and drive man! I'm going to sleep. We can figure this out in Tryon."

***

Short walks, eating Grandma's good food and just taking it easy for a couple of days. I feel like a new man; just relaxing in the swing, talking to people as they walk by.

The phone rings and Fox says, "Come on down. Let's talk to Pops about our problem."

I open the gate and Doby is all over me. "Down, boy! We ain't going for no walk today!"

Pops sticks his head out the door.

"Come around back. I have a table set up with food and some sweet tea, and we can eat and talk there."

"Pops, we used to hate it when you started one of your stories," Fox says, as we sit, "because we knew we had to listen. At the time we didn't understand each one had a life lesson that made us what we are today. Now we need another one of your stories to help us with our problem."

"Okay. Let's hear what this problem is," Pops says, as he takes a big sip of warm sake.

"We both want to join the secret service, and passed the first two tests. It's the third one we are having trouble with."

"Boy, stop running off at the mouth and tell me what your problem is," Pops says.

"We have to sleep with two different women in a two-week period in D.C. We love our women and don't want to cheat on them."

Pops is eating a chicken leg, and falls out laughing so hard he drops it. He finally stops laughing.

"Boys," he says, "why do you put so much pressure on yourselves? War calls my stories parables like in the Bible. So here is a parable for you. A young person in their teens should be a seeker of the truth and learn the lessons of life from other people's mistakes. Fox you are twenty-two and War is going on twenty-one. You cannot be a seeker your whole life. Somewhere you must find what you seek. If you haven't found it by twenty-one, you have been seeking in the wrong place. I say that to say this—you don't have a problem, you have created one. Any young man your age would give his left you-know-what to be in your shoes."

"Pops you said a lot, but I'm not quite sure I understand what you are saying," I say.

"In the Bible, Solomon was a man of God, but he had seven hundred wives and three hundred concubines on the side. He must have had some help or been one tired fellow. Abraham's wife when she got old brought him a young woman to sleep with, to have a baby. He is the father of three major religions: Christianity, Islam, and the Jewish religion, so getting a little on the side didn't hurt these two men of God.

"You two haven't sown any wild oats, mostly my fault for putting that Adam's test on you. Maybe I taught you too well to be a spiritual person, and that is a good thing. But young men and women are dying for their country in Vietnam, and you're afraid to get some on the side for yours. I ain't got nothing to do with it, but seems to me like somethin' wrong with this picture.

"Besides it's not like this is a long term thing, just a couple of times. You are grown, so I am out of your decisions. My boys will fight six men and kick their butts, jump out of a perfectly good airplane, but afraid to get a little on the side for their country. My boys done turned into monks." He starts pounding on the table and laughing out of control.

"What's so funny? This is serious and you're acting like it's a joke," I say.

"It's not funny to me, but sad. I am so proud of you two, all grown up to be spiritual young men, dedicated to your ladies. It's sad for me to think I can talk you into cheating or not cheating on them. If I can do that to you then you are not the captain of your ship. It's old Pops running your lives, not you. Did I cheat on my wife? In reality it is none of your business, any more than it's mine to know if you cheat on yours. But because you're all my boys I will tell you. Never did I cheat or even think about it, because not only was she my wife and best friend, she blessed me with a son. He blessed me with Fox and he blessed me with you, War. Why should I mess up a blessing like that for a few seconds? Excuse me, I mean a few hours of pleasure?" He looks at each of us.

"I made fun of you to show you a point. It's not what I think you should do. It's what you think you should do. Have fun, boys. This sake has me a little mellow, so, I'm going to take a nap and dream about getting some," he says, laughing as he goes inside.

"Fox it was your bright idea to come and talk with Pops. I don't know about you, but I have no idea what to do. What about you?"

"Yes I do. We worked our tails off at Bragg, had to kick three men's butts, so let's at least go to D.C. I've never been and always wanted to see the sights. As a matter of fact, let's leave tomorrow. We need all the time we have because we have no idea how to get a girl in bed, even if we want to. Neither do we know anything about D.C. So let's leave at dawn. Getting up before day at Bragg has prepared us to get up early anyway."

"Cool. See you in the a.m. Besides, we need to get away from Pops, talking about us like we're punks and scared to get some," I say.

63
Washington D.C.

"The sign says twenty-five miles to D.C. It's time to open the package Sarge gave us and see what's in it," I say to Fox.

"Okay. Let's see. There is a map of the city, with a dot showing where our hotel is, some money, two sets of car keys, a letter, and can you believe a box of rubbers?

"All that's good, but read the letter," I say.

"Greetings, Gentlemen!" Fox reads, "You have passed two difficult tests. Use your credit card whenever possible. The money is for small stuff. The cars are to drive and enjoy our city and hopefully to help you pick up girls. And the rubbers, well, I don't have to tell you what they are for. After your test is completed, I will contact you. Have fun. After two weeks with Sergeant Burns you have earned it."

"This traffic is unreal," Fox says. "The next exit is ours, and I see a park. Let's stop and take a break till this traffic dies down."

Later we drive round town and see the Lincoln Memorial, the Capitol and other places.

"There's our hotel." Fox says, "It's the Capital Hilton. Whoa, have they put us up in style? Look! There's a Polynesian restaurant. Let's stop and eat there. I've never eaten in one before."

We are sitting at a nice table by the window when this attractive Black waitress comes over and says "Aloha. My name is Mona. May I help you?"

"Mona, you sure can. We just drove here from Carolina and need a nice drink. What do you suggest?" I ask.

"Let me make a special Mai-Tai for you. It's our most popular drink. The bartender makes them for our regular costumers. Once in a while, when we're not busy and I like the customer, I make them and mine are the best this side of Hawaii. What are you fellows' names?"

"Mona, my Tai is your Tai so come on with it, and also bring us something good to eat. My buddy is called War. It's a long story; let him explain why. And I'm Fox 'cause I am sly like one."

"Nice names. I can't wait to hear how War got his name. Maybe he can tell me later," she says, smiling as she walks away.

"Looks like she got the hots for you partner," Fox says fifteen minutes later. "This is my second Mai-Tai. The island music is so romantic it makes me think of Jolene. I am getting horny for her, and have a question for you."

"Man, I am feeling no pain, listening to this mellow music and Mona is mighty friendly. I might have to hit that for real tonight. What's your question?"

"If you had to choose between killing an enemy man, and screwing an enemy woman, which would you choose?"

"That's a dumb-ass question. These Mai-Tais have me high as a Georgia pine, and of course I would screw the enemy bitch, and knock the bottom out of that thing."

"So would I, but we don't have to kill an enemy man to prove we could. Why should we have to screw some women to prove we could? Drinkin' this strong ass Mai-Tai I just made up my mind. In Russia, or even here, I will wine and dine, screw any lady I need to for the country, but just to get

245

some to prove a point they can kiss my behind. I have one of the finest ladies on earth, and a young kid, so if they can't make me a secret service agent as I am, then tough stuff."

"Here, fellows I brought you some kalua pig cooked in the old Hawaiian style for you to try. I also brought fresh Mai-Tais," Mona says putting a tray down. "Since you are from out of town, you might want to come to see Ray Charles tonight. The Genius of Soul is giving a concert at Howard University, and I know where there is a jamming party after the concert. Several of my girlfriends will be there if you are interested."

"Thanks Mona, and just think we were going to watch television tonight. We would love to see Ray, and go to a party in D.C., but are you going to be there?" I ask.

"Sure. Not only will I be there and, as I said, lots of girls will be at the after party. They've been in school studying hard for a long time and, just like me, they need a little tender loving care, if you get my drift. Two good looking boys like you with your southern accent are highly desirable. They might eat you up."

"Mona you had a nice tip coming, but now we really gonna tighten you up," Fox says.

"Hope to see y'all at the party," she smiles as she leaves.

"Blood Brother, those Tais have made you a bad brother, talking like that, but I agree with you. As I look at Mona, she is a hard working girl trying to make it through college. If I hit that thing and she falls in love with me, I would have brought much pain to her life, just for my own pleasure. Just because someone I don't even know told me to do it, because they say so. I don't think so! Besides after it's all over, I must face Jade and, like you say, I have one of the sweetest, kindest, sexiest ladies the Creator ever made. Taking care of her is a full time job, and it's so much fun."

"I'm with you. They can kiss where the sun don't shine. Let's face it, as the old ball player Dizzy Dean once said, 'If it's fact, it ain't brag.' The fact is we have trained since we were kids. We are Pops trained, and in great shape, our bodies aren't beat up from cigarettes and drugs. Therefore, we can make some serious love.

"Both of us are satisfied with our ladies so let's go see Ray tonight, skip the after party, because we might get weak with all the foxy ladies. Sleep in that fine hotel, eat like we are kings for a day, check out the Capitol building, see some old dead presidents' memorials, and head back to Carolina. Tell Pops and Big Sal we have made our decision not to sleep with any two ladies other than our own, and that's final. Do you agree?"

"I agree one hundred percent! To hell with test number three. Now, let's drop the subject and enjoy the rest of our stay in Chocolate City. As Pops says, we are grown now and captains of our ships. Let's sail this ship our way, come hell or high water."

"Hey, Mona! Bring us another round of Mai-Tais, please!" I call out.

Then to Fox I say, "We can be mellow when we see Ray, get a good night's sleep, tour, then head for Carolina and our fine ladies! You know, I hope they make us Special Agents, I could learn to love D.C., but it's up to them."

"Don't sweat it, partner, they want the best, and that's us. Drink up and let's get ready to dig us some Ray Charles."

64
Mona and Kalani

Mona comes over bringing a beautiful Hawaiian girl with long flowing hair, and a white flower in it. Her dress is short with colorful flowers like they were in Hawaii.

"Here are you drinks," Mona says. "Meet my friend, Kalani. She's the owner of the restaurant."

Fox stands up and almost falls as he staggers back into his chair.

"Wow, Mona, what you put in these Tais? They got me floating like Ali, and how do you do, Kalani. You are one fine looking young lady."

"Why, thank you," she says. "You are quite handsome yourself, and what a body you have. You must be Fox, but you don't seem sly to me. Mona suggests you ride to the concert with us. You must be tired after driving from Carolina. Plus, you don't know the city, and she thinks you had one Mai-Tai too many to be driving."

"Kalani, thank you very much. I am Fox. You are right. My buddy don't drink much and he can't hold his liquor like me. First, we have to go check in the Capital Hilton—we don't want to lose our reservations. If that's cool with you, let's ride."

"Sure. The Hilton is my favorite hotel in the city. We better leave now or we'll be late for Ray. You can leave your car in our parking lot until tomorrow. It's safe."

"Mona, they're so busy admiring each other they forget

we are here. So y'all let's go," I say.

Outside Mona pulls around in a Buick Electra 225. Fox and Kalani get in the back as I sit in the front.

"Just got this deuce and a quarter last week. Ain't she a beauty?" Mona asks.

"Sho' is. This back seat is like a living room. Hope Ray's concert is a long ways, so I can lay back and listen to this killer stereo."

We all walk in the huge lobby and up to the counter. The man behind it says, "Your keys to your suite, sir. You have a message in your room."

"Thanks," Fox says. "You ladies want to come with us while we get our messages?"

"Of course," Mona says. "We don't want you drunks falling asleep. Besides, how did that man know who you were, War, if you never been here before?"

"Come on, Mona, how many people look like me and Fox? This is our floor. Let me open the door to our suite."

"Wow! Is it because I am high, or is this the baddest room you ever seen? It has a bar, a whirlpool in the bath tub, a big TV, and water in the bed," Fox laughs, looking around.

"Come, Fox, let's go through this door into your room," Kalani says, pulling Fox by the hand.

Mona puts on Johnny Mathis singing *The Twelfth of Never.*

"This is my song. Let's dance," she says.

We dance and when the record stops we hear sounds of love-making from the other room. I can't believe Fox is getting some, but Mona has her tongue in my mouth and hand on my thing, as hard as I try to resist we end up on the water bed.

We make love off and on till morning.

Fox comes in our room and says, "Let's go. I have sinned. My head is killing me, and we never got to see Ray Charles. But Kalani made music old Ray can't top. Get up. Let's go eat."

We drop the ladies off at the restaurant.

Mona says, "Y'all come back tonight. Dinner is on the house. As a matter of fact it's at my house. I left the address on your dresser at the Hilton. See you then, love. We got to go to work. Bye for now and don't be late tonight."

***

"Forget the Hilton, dinner tonight, the statues of the Dead Presidents, and test number three. Let's head for Tryon," says Fox. "All them Mai-Tais and Kalani kissing and grinning on me, and when I tried to stop her, she asked me if I was sleeping with you, called me a punk, so I showed her I am Pops trained. Now she is in love. Says she has a million dollar house in some place called George Town. Wanted to give me a key, and asked me to move in."

"Go ahead partner, you musta put something good on her last night."

"Yeah, it was fun, but afterward I lay there watching as she slept, wishing I could leave. When I worked in Hollywood lots of people got high off cocaine. I saw coke muss up people's careers. The rumor is old Ray himself is on it. I decided under no condition would I ever try it. Sex is the same way. It's the only sin you can't do by yourself."

"Slow down, partner, stop preaching. You're beginning to sound like Pops. So what if we just got a little on the side. As a matter of fact, the ladies started it. We wanted to go see Ray. So don't feel bad. We were full of Mai-Tais, and only

250

human. But I do feel guilty when I think of Jade. The more I think of her this is my last time I cheat, because if she finds out, our relationship will never be the same. This is one time you and I both can't tell Head, Mark, and even Pops about this. You agree?"

"You better believe it. My lips are sealed. Wonder how Mona and Kalani will feel when we don't show up for dinner, or they call the hotel and can't find us. See what sex does—like coke, I never wanted to try it, because I knew I would like it. I like sex, but only with Jolene. With anyone else it's just an empty feeling after it's over. And I have to live with the guilt of cheating on her. So it just ain't worth cheating."

"Okay, partner, let's settle this once and for all. Of all the things Pops taught us, this is the one proverb I remember that relates to this time. 'A gem cannot be polished without friction, nor man without trials.' I remember that because it carried me through bad times when my leg was all jacked up. This is nothing compared to that, and as nice as those ladies are, we were not their first and won't be their last. So let's stop thinking we're God's gift to women and cheer up."

"Now we do have a problem. There's a cop car flashing for us to pull over. There a rest area. I'll pull in there."

"Gentlemen, please get out of the car with your hands where I can see them," the officer says.

"Officer, we weren't speeding. What's wrong?" I ask.

"You are under arrest for going to bed with under-age girls, and I will see to it you get at least twenty years."

"What the hell are you talking about? Those were not girls they were women over twenty one…at least they were eighteen."

Another cop gets out of the car laughing so hard he's about to cry.

"Relax fellows, it's me, Big Sal, just playing a little joke on you. You only have one more lady to sleep with, so why're you quitting? Don't you want to be agents?"

"Yes, we do very much, but we didn't sleep with those ladies last night to be some agent. We got drunk and it just happened. We are not going to try to sleep with any women just to prove a point, so I guess our agent days are over," Fox say.

"On the contrary, here is a contract with all the information you need. Fill it out. I will pick it up in Tryon next week. Mona was one of our agents and we wanted to know if either one of you is a good lover, since you might have to seduce someone. You might want to know I asked her where you were on the chart in the love-making department. I laughed when she said you were off the chart. Her friend Kalani told her Fox put something on her that blew her mind. Mona wants to help break you in. So drive safely boys! Go home, read over the papers, sign up and get ready for some big time adventures."